FEARED TO SPEAK

JACK TENOR

I dedicate this book to all people in the world who fought against the Nazis and their regime during the dark days of occupation. Thank you for all you did for us.

Jack Tenor

TABLE OF CONTENT

Chapter 1

I begged the universe that no one got killed today. Not by me, at least. The sharp, late summer sun reflected from the windows of the buildings on the opposite side of the channel, blinding me. I squinted. Nice weather in Amsterdam after a period of rain.

I stepped inside the bookstore and closed the door behind me. The strong, sour-sweet stench of old books smashed the back of my nose, and I restrained the urge to sneeze it out. On the door's frame hung an old bell without a heart. It wiggled, sending a silent ring-ring to nowhere. I loved books, reading whenever possible and spending hours in bookstores and libraries.

"Good morning, sir. How can I help you?" The bookseller's voice came from behind the counter.

I walked toward his voice. The dark silhouette got a face. A tall bald man in his thirties wore an expensive but old suit in shades of grey. Everything was grey here: the floor, the shelves, the cold, damp air. I opened my mouth, but the screeching of brakes made me turn around. A car stopped in front of the store.

The door opened, and a man in an SS uniform strode toward the counter, ignoring me. At the counter, he clacked his heels and raised his right hand.

"*Heil Hitler!*" A small piece of ceiling paint chipped off and flew in a perfect spiral down.

"I'm looking for the book *The Travel Diary of a Philosopher* by Hermann von Keyserling. Do you have it?" he said in German with a strong Hessian dialect.

The bookseller stood petrified, losing his ability to speak. A statue would have envied his posture. And the paleness of his face—no marble could compete with it.

The officer locked his sights on the bookseller and stood there for a while. Then he raised his voice. "Do you understand what I'm asking you?"

A woman's head with long dark hair stuck out of the shadows between two bookcases. Sophie, the young wo-man who had sent me a message to meet her here. She gazed at me, sending questions through her eyes, but I shook slightly my head. *Not today, Sophie. Today we will play a little game.*

"I'm sorry, *Herr Obersturmführer.* I don't have any travelogues," I said in German, trying not to gaze at Sophie, who hid herself back in the shadows.

He turned at me, measuring me from feet to the head. "You speak German. That's great. Which part of Ger-many are you from?"

"I'm sorry, *Herr Obersturmführer*, I was born here in Amsterdam."

"That explains your accent. You sound like from the village at boundaries."

"Yes. But I noticed you're from Frankfurt, aren't you?"

"Excellent observation! So, you don't have Keyserling's book?"

"No. I sell classics. Schiller, Goethe, and others. If you liked it, I have a delightful collection of Karl May's books."

"You have my respect. And what happened to him?" He pointed at the bookseller.

"He's my older brother," I lied, "He's a deaf-mute man. This is our shop, and I'm taking care of him. Parents passed away a long time ago."

"You're a German, and you take care of your disabled brother? You're a hero, *Herr...*"

"Müller. Maximilian."

"I am *Obersturmführer* Herman von Dahrt."

We shook hands.

"It is sad you don't have that book, *Herr* Schniedler. Everyone recommends it. I'm leaving for Berlin in two hours and have nothing to read on the train. Never mind. I need to go."

"It definitely is a great book. I'd like to read it myself. Let me accompany you to the door, *Herr Obersturmführer*, so my talking will not make you miss your train."

"A hero and a gentleman. It was an honor to meet you!"

"The honor was mine, *Herr Oberstumführer* von Dahrt."

I took him by his elbow. He was taller than me. Everyone was taller than me. I didn't give a shit.

Reaching the door, I opened it and said goodbye to him. He clacked his heels and raised his hand again as if I was interested. I held the rear car door for him, and he installed himself on the seat. The driver had kept the engine running. I stood on the sidewalk for a while, watching the car strolling away. At the corner, the officer looked through the open window, and I waved, grinning like a basket of apples. He waved back, and the car disappeared.

I returned to the store. Sophie stood next to the bookseller, stroking his back.

"It's all right, Daan. He's gone," she said in a low voice.

He sighed, gazing at me.

"My name is Erik Jansen," I said, stretching my hand.

"I'm Daan Vermeulen. I don't know how to thank you, Erik," he said, accepting my hand.

"Don't mention it, Daan," I said.

"I've often imagined how it would be when someone like him entered my store. I've imagined how I would spit into his face. But now? I feel embarrassed."

"Don't mention it. Don't think about it, all right? There's nothing to feel embarrassed for." I nodded at the woman. "Hi, Sophie."

"Hi, Erik," she said. She wore a light blue summer dress with no decoration, and I liked its simplicity. Sophie was fit, tall, and remarkably pretty.

I raised my eyebrows, flashing at the bookseller.

She waved her hand. "You can talk. Daan knows," she said.

"What do I know?" Daan said.

"About me, Daan."

"Oh, yes. I'm sorry. I don't feel good. If you'll excuse me, I'll leave you and make coffee so you can talk freely." He spun on one foot and strolled toward the green curtain with tiny white and yellow flowers hanging in the corner. "I'll make a cup for myself as well. I need it like never before," he said while walking.

I waited for him to pull back the curtain, and when he did, it revealed a comfy kitchenette corner.

Sophie giggled and hugged me. "So good to see you, Erik."

"I'm happy, too. Sorry I led that SS pig out, but today is a nice and sunny day, and I didn't want to see the blood."

"How did you know I would kill him? What if I just did the same as you did?"

"Because you kill everyone in a Nazi uniform, Sophie."

"That's not true."

5

"Since you've been playing this secret game of yours, it is. Someday, someone will write a book about you. I believe that."

"Secret game?" She pounded on the counter. "I'm an agent if you didn't notice."

"No, you're not. You're an assassin."

Water boiled, and cups rattled.

"Just like you."

"I can't believe you said that. Like me?" I grinned. Sophie let herself be hired by the gray eminence for hard-to-do tasks. She liked to act as a hooker, and then she killed the target, showing no mercy. Rumors had it she never put her homeland in danger. She'd always acted outside of Amsterdam, outside of the Netherlands.

She said nothing, but her eyes lit up with wild flames. No way she was killing for money. This lady enjoyed killing Nazis, and she was splendidly good at it.

"All right. Enough flattery. Why am I here?" I said.

Daan returned, carrying a tray with two steaming cups, a saucer with a few sugar cubes, and a lovely porcelain teapot. "I don't know if you drink black or white, with or without sugar."

"Black, no sugar. Thank you."

"That's good. I don't need to return for milk. Don't mind the teapot, please. I have no other pot, and coffee tastes good from it."

He put the tray on the counter and nodded at Sophie. I put the cup to my lips and took a sip. The coffee tasted excellent.

"Where did you buy this coffee, Daan?"

"Oh, it's an Italian blend. Sophie brought it directly from Milan."

"From Milan? Interesting. I must admit I've never drunk coffee from Milan."

"Do you like it?" He beamed like a student getting his first kiss.

"Very much."

He nodded and turned away from me. Then turned back and away again. I put my hand on his shoulder. He smiled. I'd never seen such a confused and distracted person.

"Erik," Sophie said, stepping closer, "I'd like to ask if you could accompany me to the NSB reception tonight."

"What?"

"I'd like to ask you…"

"No, I understood. Why me?"

"I trust you, and you are good at improvisation."

"But I'm bad at running away from the crime scene. If you kill one of them, I will be the first interrogated person."

"I need a private eye beside me," she said.

"But NSB? Those primitive collaborants? How many SS officers will be there?"

She stepped closer and put her hand on my shoulder. "No killing. I promise."

"Sorry, Sophie, I don't believe it."

She pulled her mouth into an adorable smile and widened her maroon eyes, locking them on me. I sighed and drank more coffee, trying to avoid her gaze. At that moment, I understood how dangerous she was.

"Erik, please."

"I hate you, Sophie."

"No. You love me. But you're too shy to admit it."

"Anyone who loved you ended up dead."

She kissed my cheek and giggled with the sweetest sound I had ever heard. The last sound a person would listen to before falling dead. Sophie wasn't just a killer, but she was an artistic killer, making her victims look forward to being killed. Goosebumps developed on my forearms.

"All right, Sophie. I'll go with you. But, please, never ever laugh in the way you just did when I'm around. Never!"

Chapter 2

The collar of the borrowed white shirt pressed against my neck, strangling me. I stood in the corner of the ballroom in the palace built in Watergraafsmeer, sticking my fingers under the collar and pulling it away from my neck. The shirt was two numbers above my size, but its collar must have shrunk from frequent washing. I borrowed it with the tuxedo from a friend. Oxford shoes as well. The mighty universe must have liked me a lot, for the shoes were comfortable and fit my feet.

"I will rip this collar off the shirt, I swear," I whispered while righting my tie.

"No, please, don't do that," Sophie said. A nonchalant smile sat on her face, displaying cute dimples in her cheeks. An angelic daemon.

No one could tell how I hated to be here, wearing clothes I detested and pretending to be someone I wasn't among the people I would spit on if I met any of them on the street at night. Sophie, on the other hand, looked very relaxed and calm. She wore a lovely white gown tight enough to highlight her narrow waist. In her hand she held a black leather purse so small I didn't believe she could've put so much as a handkerchief in it. I would've bet the purse hid a sharp knife, though. Sophie's long dark hair fell across her shoulders like a light breeze. From time to time, she tucked a strand of hair behind her ear with hands covered in opera gloves.

"Can I go home?" I said. "I escorted you here as I promised. You no longer need me."

"Erik, please, calm down. I need you here."

She cast a mother-like gaze at me, reached out, and twisted my collar. It felt better.

"You look good. Just calm down a bit. Everything will be fine," she said.

"No, it won't." I waved my hand around. "Look at what is happening here. The room is full of people I don't like."

I gazed around. The palace was old and could have been built two hundred years ago. I would have bet it had belonged to some noble family who had used it as a summer house. Those NSB suckers must have deported them or forced them to leave. How many balls had been organized here before? How many happy people?

The ballroom was vast, easily accommodating a hundred guests or more. Large marble tiles formed the floor. The wide stairs led up to the gallery, supported by twelve pillars standing along all four walls. Behind the pillars, heavy tables bent under the load of serving bowls full of cuts of meat, sauces, and fruits. Some fruits were exotic. I'd never seen them in my life. This feast could feed several poor families for a few days. Heavy red curtains with golden ties decorated the balustrades. Three crystal chandeliers, each the size of a small truck, hung from the ceiling, casting bright light. Through the windows in the gallery, darkness was already spreading outside. The hands of the enormous, gilded clock hanging above the stairs showed the time as nine o'clock in the evening.

A bead of sweat ran from between my shoulder blades along my spine, finding its way right between my buttocks. Awful feeling. I suppressed the urge to touch my butt. The ballroom was overheated. I felt a warm draft. They must have the heating on. Strange, though. It was summer, for God's sake. Why didn't these pricks open the window? I couldn't stop shaking my head over the massive waste of money for the collaborant elites while the ordinary people had to think twice before buying a loaf of bread. It pissed me off. It always had.

I took two glasses of champagne from the tray carried by a waiter striding around me and handed one to Sophie. She accepted it, and we cheered. It tasted like piss. I would bet it was the most expensive champagne in the world. Or someone had bought the cheapest one and sold it like the most expensive champagne. Most likely the truth. These people couldn't recognize the difference. Filthy parasites.

"Look at them," I said. "They act like millionaires but don't serve proper drinks. One more dose of these bubbles, and I will fly up to the ceiling like a balloon."

She giggled. "You would rather have a shot of Scotch, right?"

"I do prefer the Scotch." I swallowed the rest of the bubbly liquid and shivered. "If they don't serve Glenlivet in thirty minutes, I'm going home."

"I'll ask for one if you need it so desperately."

"Good idea." I grinned. "If we're pretending you're my sister, you should get some for me."

"All right. Wait here, *Herr* Maximilian Müller, or what name you have come up with."

"Müller, yes. The same I said to that Nazi monkey this morning. That story worked, why to change it?"

She nodded. "I liked that story you told him, and I like to play your sister."

"Hey, sis, where's my whisky?"

"Give it a few moments. I'm sending signals to that handsome waiter." She nodded toward the bloke in the black trousers and white shirt juggling an empty tray between the groups of standing people.

"Oh, a new admirer? Should I be concerned, sis?"

"Don't worry about me. He's handsome, but I don't like him."

"I'm not worried about you. I'm worried about him," I said, laughing.

She said nothing but hit my shoulder with her clenched fist.

"Ouch! That wasn't nice."

"Next time, it'll be worse," she said and tilted her head back, laughing a laugh that could melt the ice on the North Pole.

I touched her shoulder and nodded toward the fat man who had just entered the hall. "Look, Edward Vinke."

"Oh, mister mayor. Gosh, how I hate him. That pig made a quick career."

"Like most of the others. Just wash your hands thoroughly after you touch any of them."

"Why?"

"Because they are stuck deeply in the Nazi arses. Your hands will get dirty."

She giggled, covering her mouth with her palm. More people began to enter. The most privileged few. Yesterday, most of them had begged for a piece of bread. Now, they were at the top of the top. They knew the correct boots to lick.

They posed for photographers. Tomorrow's newspapers would be full of their faces. Seeing them shaking hands in the bright light of the reflectors installed for this occasion made me want to bury myself far away from these snakes.

Sophie stepped closer to me and hooked her arm through mine. "Do you know that man? That whose wife wears the yellow dress?" She waved slightly her free hand.

"Who wouldn't know him? He used to live near Vondelpark but then moved to Jordaan when his shop was bankrupted. I went to school with his son. He wasn't a bad person. His son, I mean. Who knows how he's now."

She gazed at me with her mouth open. "Bankrupted? Really? I didn't know that. Now, he's the supreme supplier of apples for the *Wehrmacht*."

"Apples? What would the *Wehrmacht* need apples for? Instead of grenades?"

"Who cares? For him, the only important thing is he gets his money." Sophie giggled.

"Something is rotten in the state of The Netherlands."

"Something? Everything! Look at that man." She pointed her finger at one guest I didn't recognize, who was standing there alone, sad, and scared.

"So? What's with him?"

"He's a well-known local loyalist. A professor at the lyceum and a member of some local committee. When they asked him the first time to join their party, he refused. Then, they seized his wife and two children and held them in prison until he agreed. The party needs him because he has a big influence on people. Now he has his family back."

"That's a sad story, indeed," I said.

Sophie turned her gaze to me. Her face was so serious that I was concerned about her health. I'd never seen her like that. That sudden surge of emotions. I shivered. It would kill her one day. She sipped the champagne.

"They use their power to spread fear. That secures their position. It's easier to be feared than loved." Another sip.

"When they seized his children and wife, no one helped him. No one," she continued in a sad voice.

"Well, I don't care if they use fear to strengthen their position. I will never bend my back for them," I said and questioned myself, letting the view haze. It was easy to say it, even to say it loudly. But would I stand by my word in any situation? If someone blackmailed me, threatening my close relatives?

Sophie said nothing, didn't even look at me.

"Excuse me," the deep male voice said.

I startled. Sophie yanked my arm.

"I accidentally overheard your conversation," the man said.

He could be in his forties and wore a black tuxedo like we all did. His face was pale and wrinkled. The glass of champagne he held trembled. He hadn't touched it. It was still full. This man was taller than me by a head. And as thin as if he hadn't eaten for years. The tuxedo hung on him.

"And you are?" I said.

"Dawid Kuipers."

I said my fake name and introduced Sophie as my sister. We shook hands. His palm was sweaty and slipped from my grip when I released it a bit.

"I accidentally overheard your conversation," he repeated, tilting his head down.

"So what?"

"I just… I think I have something to tell you." He lifted his head but avoided direct eye contact.

"I'm afraid I don't understand. Who are you? What are you doing for a living?"

"I'm the principal of the elementary school."

"Look, Mr…"

"Kuipers. Dawid Kuipers."

"Mr. Kuipers, how did you end up at this reception?"

"Me? Jan Mussert invited me."

"The local leader of the NSB?"

"Yes."

"So, you have a good relationship with the NSB."

His eyes widened. "No! I'm here because I don't want to get into trouble. They would destroy me if I didn't. I need to take care of the children at our school, you know? Protect them."

Sophie and I locked eyes for a moment. This was ridiculous. We burst into laughter.

Dawid Kuipers shrank and took two steps away from us as if he wanted to show the others that he didn't belong to us.

When we stopped, he stepped back.

"You're young. Full of enthusiasm. That will change when you reach a certain age." He made the face of a stern professor talking down to a pupil. That stamped on my temperament.

"It has nothing to do with age. Look at you! The principal of the school. I bet you have changed your attitude, and now, you teach children how awesome it is to be a Nazi or a Nazi bootlicker like anywhere in the country. And, behind the curtain, you claim how you hate them. Doesn't it sound like a hypocrisy to you?"

His cheeks reddened. "I have never…"

I interrupted him. "You do exactly what others do, and that's your excuse. You shit your pants every morning you wake up and realize you have to go to work. You are embarrassed by it and want everyone to be like you so you can feel better." My voice lowered to whispering. "Now, say what you want to tell, or leave us alone!"

His cheeks reddened more. A thick vein developed on his forehead.

"Look, young man." His face changed into the face of the lion talking to its prey. He leaned closer to my ear. "I know who you are, Erik Jansen!" he whispered. "I know you very well. You are the son of the former Senior Constable who died a few months ago."

I clenched my fists.

He went on. "Now, listen carefully, Erik. In thirty minutes, you will come up with a generous offer, or I will reveal your true identity to the first SS officer I meet. Do you understand?"

Dawid Kuipers took three steps backward and bowed his head lightly at Sophie, accelerating toward the group of people who looked like him.

Sophie stepped closer. "What now?"

"Now?" I sighed. "Now, I have to kill him."

Chapter 3

A waiter appeared by my side. He carried a tray with a single glass on it, half full of golden liquid. He offered it to me, and I took the glass, lifting it closer to my nose. The well-known aroma entered, tickling, and smiling at me—Scotch. And a good one.

"That's from that lady. She thought this would please you," the waiter said, nodding toward the woman wearing red.

Anna Bakker cheered with her glass of champagne. I cheered back, grinning at her. She dragged on the cigarette, releasing a gray-blue cloud.

Her shoulder-cut blonde hair was adorned with a red barrette which emphasized her blue eyes. She wore a narrow-waisted, red jacket paired with well-fitted red trousers—not very common for our times, yet so elegant. I'd always liked it. No one knew what exactly she was doing. Rumor had it she worked for the Dutch secret service or the government in exile. Others said she led the resistance. I didn't care about any of that. She was my patron.

"Sophie, you didn't tell me Anna would be here," I said with reprehension in my voice.

"Oh, I'm sorry, Erik, I thought I did. I came here to meet with her."

What was Anna doing among these collaborators? I would bet my hands she was up to something. I had to talk to her. My problem with Dawid Kuipers might disrupt her intentions. She was a bit of a dark horse, so it was better to tell her what had just happened. I strolled toward her.

"Erik!" A voice stopped me.

I turned around and grinned. This was a day full of astonishment. Simon, the man who once saved my life, the man who led the local resistance, was grinning back.

"Shhh, here I'm Maximilian Müller, a German bookseller born in Amsterdam. What are you doing here?"

He circled with his hand. "I'm a part of this."

"A part?"

He leaned closer to my ear. "Well, I have to explain a few things. I'm sorry Anna didn't... Never mind," he whispered. "This is my cover. In the eyes of these people, I'm a manufacturer of metal screws and bolts, supplying the *Wehrmacht*."

"Come on!"

"How do you think I finance the resistance?"

What? He let the Nazis to finance the resistance. What a clever move!

"All right," I said. "And Anna?"

"She will tell you when she wants to." He stepped back. "Come, I will introduce you to a few SS officers. That might help you in the future." And he grabbed me by my shoulder and led me to the nearest group of men wearing SS uniforms.

"Gentlemen," he said in German. All faces turned at us. I swallowed.

"This young man is a future star within our society. *Herr* Maximilian Müller, a bookseller."

The Nazi heads nodded, and they continued in discussion, not showing interest. One officer separated from the group and stepped closer.

"*Herr* Müller, do you have a bookstore in Amsterdam?" he said.

"Yes, I do."

"Do you have, by any chance, *The Travel Diary of a Philosopher* by Hermann von Keyserling?"

"I'm sorry, but I don't have that title. It seems to be very popular. Actually, today, I had a visitor, my friend *Obersturmführer* Herman von Dahrt, who asked for the same book."

His face brightened. "He was there?"

"Yes, before he left for Berlin."

"Oh, yes, he had to leave. He's a very powerful SS investigator in Berlin. He mentioned a kind young man but forgot to tell your name." The officer turned to the group. "*Kameraden*, this is a good friend of *Obersturmführer* Herman von Dahrt!"

Now, all the Nazis grinned. Everyone shook my hand. I heard a shower of German names and ranks. Everyone asked some questions about the well-being of my family as if they knew me. My consciousness turned off, and my thoughts focused on the wish to have a grenade. How much it would have eased the world if I had gotten rid of them? The rush of their enthusiasm went on. I knew they were just playing a game, pretending their interest in me. Each of them wanted to make me his friend because of *Obersturmführer*. In other words, those bastards licked my boots.

Sophie approached.

"Gentlemen," I said. "This is my sister *Fräulein* Sofia Müller."

Sophie curtsied. Everyone forgot I existed, and they surrounded her, praising her age and beauty. I expected her to pull a knife out and cut their throats. She would do it in a second, and I wouldn't mind. The blood could disappear from a black gown with one washing only.

I gazed at Simon, who grinned from ear to ear. He winked at me. Perhaps he knew her; perhaps he didn't. It didn't matter. I suspected that he had the same thoughts as I did.

I left them there and headed toward Anna again. She'd already gone away from where I'd seen her. Glancing around, I found her at a table with food. I beseeched the mighty universe for no other people to stop me and strolled under the gallery.

As I walked, my eyes locked with Dawid Kuipers' eyes. He raised two fingers and gave me a rapid head tilt. I got the message. Twenty minutes left, and time was run-ning out.

Anna held a beautifully crafted porcelain plate and, with a silver fork, loaded with pork chops on it. I took another plate from the stack at the end of the table and pretended to be interested in Prosciutto di Parma, served on a huge silver tray, and accompanied by Gorgonzola cheese.

"Hello, Anna," I whispered as I got closer to her.

"Don't need to whisper. I've already acknowledged I know you," she said in her normal voice.

"Thank you for the Scotch."

"You're welcome."

"I'm here with Sophie, you know?"

She straightened her back and cast a gaze at me, one that would make most men run away.

"First, I spotted you and sent you whiskey. So, yes, I knew you were here. Second, I advised Sophie to ask you to escort her."

I said nothing but laughed in my mind. This was Anna Bakker. The only person in the world who knew how to manage me. I liked her.

Someone attracted my attention. Dawid Kuipers. He dared to lock eyes with me.

"Is something wrong with you, Erik?" Her face exposed genuine concerns.

I sighed. "My cover is breaking apart."

"Go on!" Anna reached with her hand again and poured brown gravy over the pork chops. It smelled of junipers and garlic.

I told her about Dawid Kuipers and his attempt to blackmail me.

"I need to kill him," I said.

She stopped for a while, her hand with the sauce boat frozen above her plate. Then she shrugged and poured another portion of the sauce over her plate. A light grin sat on her face, but her eyes spoke of a serious situation.

"I like this sauce. My mother used to cook it. Juniper adds a fresh kick to it."

I waited. This wasn't her normal reaction. This meant she was thinking. I guessed the incident might interrupt her plan, whatever it was.

"Kuipers could jeopardize your intention, couldn't he?"

She said nothing.

"Could he reveal your true identity as well?"

She shook her head.

"Simon's?"

Another shake of the head.

"Then? Does it have something to do with Sophie? Why is she here?"

"The less you know, the better for you. And for us," she said. I'd heard this often from her. She was right. If something terrible happened and the SS or the Gestapo interrogated me, I would rather know nothing. Their interrogation methods were full of pain and made people sing out everything they knew. And everything they didn't know but thought they knew. Even small, already forgotten details that had happened twenty years ago.

"He knows nothing about me, Simon, or Sophie, so don't worry," Anna continued. "Now it is important to restore your cover. I saw you making friends among the SS officers. That's good. You can use it in the future. It's worth not destroying it before you profit from it. It's worth not to destroy what you have already achieved."

I understood what she was talking about. Since we had cooperated, my task had been to pretend to be someone else, build new connections, and use this advantage to gain critical information that helped to increase interest. Now, everything was in danger.

"You should get rid of him. Considering your new acquaintances, I think you would win if you used your reputation against his reputation. But he will spill the beans before the NSB. And that's what we must prevent from happening."

"Should I…"

"No, killing him here and now wouldn't be wise. What would we do if any of these people found his dead body?"

With deliberate slowness, she took a bite and savored the combination of mashed potatoes and sauce.

"No," she said. "Spoil his plan. Prevent him from speaking. Take him out of here. Beat him. Tie him. I don't care. Just get rid of him. Later, I will send someone to ask him some questions. He might know something useful."

"All right. I will respect your wishes."

I returned the empty plate to the heap and walked away. Nothing could stop some unpleasant things that were going to happen to Dawid Kuipers.

My eyes sought Sophie with no success. She'd disappeared into thin air. The group of SS officers occupied the same place as before, but she wasn't among them. Several couples danced to the rhythm of a waltz played by a string quintet. I could only guess she had taken care of her task or gone to the toilet. If there were any toilets.

Without her, I had to improvise. The best would be to lure Dawid Kuipers into the shadow place and beat him until he fainted. When I'd come here, I'd spotted, through the opened door, a dark corridor leading to the back of the building. That door was in the corner of the ballroom. I disliked that idea. This was supposed to be a nice day, not a bloody break-some-jaws day. But I had no other options.

I stood fifteen feet away from him. He was talking to somebody I didn't know. A bald man in a black tuxedo. For a moment, I thought I'd seen him before, but it was just my imagination playing those strange games with me. I coughed loudly enough to be heard in New York. The giant ballroom muffled the sound and absorbed it to zero. No one turned their head at me. No one cared.

But it worked for Kuipers. He lifted his head and cast a questioning gaze at me. I tilted my head aside and strolled toward the door, not paying attention to whether he would follow.

Ten steps before the door, I bumped into the waiter. He carried an empty silver tray. I doubted he was older than me.

I grabbed him by his arm and said, "Where does that door lead?"

"Which door?"

I pointed at it. "That door."

"Oh, that door. To the corridor."

"All right. That's very useful. And where does the corridor lead?"

"To the stables."

"Stables? A bit strange, isn't it?"

"I heard that in the past, the king used to ride into the ballroom on his horse."

"King? Here? Perhaps a drunk sailor."

He chuckled and shrugged. "I've just heard it."

"All right. Thank you."

He lifted his leg to take a step, but I stopped him again.

"Wait!"

"Yes?"

"Is it used often?"

He looked scared, pressing the empty tray to his chest.

"You're an SS officer?"

"Do I look like an SS officer? Do I wear the uniform?"

"I don't know."

"Come on! No danger from me. I sell books."

He scanned people around us. Everyone stood more than ten feet away. He stepped closer to me.

"There is one thing…"

"Yes?"

"The officers. The SS officers sometimes take girls there. You know what for, right?" He winked. "It's very dark there."

"Sure. That's what I want to do as well. Thanks!"

I patted him on his back, and he continued toward the kitchen. Dawid Kuipers approached. A mocking smile sat on his face. *Not for a long time, Dawid, don't worry.*

"Did you come up with something?" he said.

"Yes. Follow me!" I turned and took a few steps toward the door. He followed. Grabbing the handle, I opened it and turned back to him. He stood still. I waved my hand in an invitation gesture. He shook his head.

I glanced inside. The light from the ballroom gleamed in, revealing the walls and floor at the beginning of the corridor. Like the mouth of a hungry beast.

"Are you afraid?" I said, grinning at him.

"I won't go inside."

"Why?"

"I just won't. Tell me what you have here and now."

"All right," I nodded, closing the door. "The thing is that I'm not permitted to promise you anything."

"Then we have nothing to talk about. Prepare for torture." He spun on one foot.

"Wait!" I jumped next to him and grabbed his shoulder, turning him back. He didn't resist.

"Let me finish. I can't. But there is a man waiting for us who can. And will."

He hesitated for a few moments, tilting his head down. I couldn't say what thoughts passed his mind.

"He will be generous," I said.

He lifted his head. "How much?"

"You won't have to work for the rest of your life."

His eyes widened, and his chest heaved. He pulled the white handkerchief out of his pocket and wiped the sweat from his forehead with a trembling hand.

"This is what you were waiting for, right? And now it is happening, so don't be stupid and grab this opportunity with both hands."

He sighed. "All right then. Who is he?"

"You'll see. I don't want to say it aloud here. Hurry up!"

I opened the door again, and he slipped in, followed by me. The door closed without making much noise. Darkness replaced the light from the chandeliers and surrounded us. I scanned the handle with my fingers, hoping for a key sticking out. There was nothing. Never mind. I would take the risk. If any of the officers appeared by accident, I would eliminate them, too.

"Where is he?" Dawid Kuipers said. His voice echoed strangely in the corridor.

"Just walk. You'll see the light."

I heard his steps in front of me. He moved slowly. The music echoing from the ballroom faded out. My eyes began to get used to the darkness. This would be enough. I jumped beside him like a leopard and grabbed him by his shoulders. Rotating on one foot, I smashed him on the wall with all my strength. It rumbled. I guessed he hit the wall with his head, but I lost contact with him. His breath came from down there, heavy and jerky.

I bent over, reaching with both hands. A sudden pain flashed from my left shoulder. That bastard kicked me with his knee. I felt the touch of the fabric of his trousers. The unexpected energy knocked me to the cold floor. I pushed on my hands, eager to get up, but my shoulder protested and sent a new portion of sharp pain. It took my breath away, and, for a couple of seconds, I couldn't take in any air. Getting on my knees,

I gathered all my strength and took a deep breath. It made the sound of a drowning man.

Dawid Kuipers coughed and panted. I jumped in that direction, landing my hands on his body. He began to kick, moving his legs as if he was pedaling a bicycle. It didn't help, though. A series of short punches into his belly and chest calmed him down. He yelped in pain. I grabbed the collar of his tuxedo and got to my feet, pulling him up. He was like a giant, limp rag doll. I nailed him on the wall.

"Listen carefully, you piece of shit," I said, breathing into his face. "What you did wasn't fair, and you are going to pay a very high price for it."

The rag doll came alive, and he broke free from my grip, running deeper into the corridor. I didn't hesitate and leaped behind him. Not knowing where I was headed, I ran through the blackness. I heard his panting in front of me. He wasn't far away. I stretched my hand out, and my fingers slipped on his tuxedo.

This part of the corridor was less dark. I saw the contours of a white door on the wall. The white color shone with a dull glow. I spotted the silhouette of Dawid Kuipers six or seven feet before me. He ran, wobbling and waving with his hands like a windmill. I added more energy to my muscles. This would end quickly.

A white figure appeared next to the door and rammed into him. He fell to the floor.

"Don't crash into me, Erik!"

Sophie!

I barely stopped.

"What are you doing here?" I said in between pants.

"Helping."

"Yeah, thanks!"

I bent over Dawid Kuipers' body. He lay on his belly, so I turned him over. He didn't react, his muscles lax, and his limbs hanging.

"Don't play the rag doll again, Kuipers!" I slapped him hard.

My hands got wet. I felt it. I straightened my back and raised them closer to my face. The metallic scent kicked my nose.

"What the…"

"I had to do it, Erik," Sophie said in a low voice.

"Do what?"

"Kill him. I drove the knife right into his chest. He fell down dead."

"Oh, for God's sake!"

Bending again over his dead body, I spotted a dark stain developing on the white shirt, right on his chest. Yes, this bloke was dead before he hit the floor. I wiped the blood from my palms onto his tuxedo. He didn't mind, and I didn't either. Now, it didn't matter. We were going to face more severe problems than my dirty hands. I straightened my back and gazed at Sophie's shadow.

"Sophie, now, we are completely fucked up."

Chapter 4

"Why?" said Sophie.

"Why? Because he wasn't supposed to die."

"I don't think so. He was a collaborator."

"Yes, he was, but the investigation could lead to Anna or Simon."

"Who will investigate the death of this filthy pig?"

"Anyone. His death could ruin everything. We have to hide his body."

"But why would we do that? We can just leave him here. No one will ever enter this dark corridor."

Her voice lowered. The glare reflected from her eyes in the darkness as if she were in a trance.

"Actually, you're wrong. The Nazi officers bring drunken girls here to have fun."

"Anna will be mad, right?" she said after a while.

I gazed around, but there was nothing to see. Light. I needed a light. Stretching my hands before me, I stepped to the white doors. There was no handle on them. I pushed against the doors, but they didn't move.

"Sophie, don't you have matches?"

"No, not here."

"We must drag him further."

A door slammed. Someone entered the corridor and walked toward us. I didn't like it. Sophie touched my arm. I could tell she was preparing her knife for another action. The yellow circle in the distance was moving toward us. Something was wrong. Who would use an electric flashlight during a quickie? I took Sophie's hand and pulled her back. Now wasn't the time for ruthless killing. Not an SS officer. I had to talk to him. Convince him I had a girl here, wanting to have fun. Ask him for a favor to wait outside. If he resisted, then I would jump on him and pacify him with a bunch of carefully aimed punches.

My blood pressure went up. Taking two deep breaths, my heartbeat calmed. I was ready for action.

I stepped forward, leaving Sophie behind and coughing so he would notice my presence.

"Erik! Where are you?"

It was Simon. Relief.

"Simon," Sophie whispered, "we are here."

The flashlight's circle came closer, reflecting on our faces. Then it lit on the spot with the dead body.

"What the hell happened here?!" Simon said.

"An accident," I said.

"I see. You had nothing better to do, right?"

"I will not apologize for killing this dirty collaborant," Sophie said, shaking her head.

In the light of the flashlight, I glanced at her white gown. Blood splashed over it.

"You can't go back like this," I said, pointing at her.

"You can't go either. Your hands are crimson with blood," Simon said and handed me his handkerchief.

I looked at my hands. They were still smeared with blood. The handkerchief didn't help. I peered at Sophie.

"See what you've done?" I said.

"I'm telling you again, I won't apologize."

"I don't expect your apologies. Just, please, admit that it wasn't a wise move."

Simon observed us, skipping his gaze from one to another.

"No need to apologize or do fancy things," he said. "He got what he deserved."

I opened my mouth to explain what Anna and I had agreed on, but he interrupted me.

"Don't say a word. I don't care. It is how it is, and we are going to solve this."

Sophie gazed at me. Her eyes were full of reproach. I kept my mouth shut. Whatever I said would stand against me. The last thing we needed was to argue with each other.

"I see what happened between you two," Simon continued. "But don't worry, things aren't as bad as you thought. Now, help me with this bloke."

I grabbed Dawid Kuipers by his legs, and Simon took care of the rest. The dead body was heavy, as if made of stones.

"Sophie, take the flashlight and light our way."

It didn't go easy. I staggered under the weight of the dead body. It was pushing me down. Despite the lit floor, I saw nothing. Simon suffered just like me, being in a worse position because he was walking backward.

"Where are we going?" I said, pushing words through my clenched teeth.

"I have a car with a driver at the stables. He'll take care of this."

Huffing and tripping, we made it to the back of the corridor. The wall had windows now, and the glare of the late-night sky sharpened the contours of objects in the corridor. Peering through the window, I spotted the car outside.

We approached the double door installed right at the end and put the body down. Simon asked Sophie to open it. The door wasn't locked. He disappeared but returned in no time with a man I didn't know. He wore casual dark trousers and a white shirt like an ordinary man. Like anyone else who just happened to be outside.

"Sami will take care of this problem," Simon said.

"I'm not sure if I will. I told you that I'm here to back you. If I go away, you might be in danger."

"That's nice, but we would be all in danger if someone found this bloke."

"That bloke can't speak."

"Do you think it will bother those NSB bootlickers? They would want to show off in front of SS officers spreading terror. I knew Dawid Kuipers. He was distant family to the mayor. Can you imagine what would happen?"

"Yes, I can imagine it. But right now, I need to stay here. You know what for." He shook his head. "Not mentioning a curfew violation. If someone catches me…"

"That's an order, soldier!" Simon's face changed. His eyes were full of energy. His voice didn't accept refusals. He stalked toward the car without looking back.

Sami swallowed and nodded at me. "Help me to put him into the car's trunk."

I bent and grabbed the legs.

"Not you!" Simon said, handing me a huge bottle full of some liquid he brought from the car. "You wash your hands and get back. Tell Anna what happened. She needs to know."

I hesitated. I didn't want to go back. The idea of pretending to be a good fella with those traitors pressed on my chest. Simon understood my reluctance.

"No one else can go there now, Erik. Sophie's dress has changed color. I'll also be back, but I can't speak to her. You have blood only on your hands."

I nodded. The bottle was full of pure water. I washed my hands and left them there. When I returned, the ballroom had changed. Less couples danced than before. More drunken heads. Men released their ties or put them away. Wives stood on the gallery, observing their husbands from a distance as they flirted with single women. Or perhaps they were hookers. I didn't care.

Anna stood nearby, talking to an SS officer. She smiled, but it was just a grimace painted on her face. I knew her. Her eyes were cold. She calculated each move of her hands and each step she took.

I strolled behind the SS officer, looking away from her and heading to the buffet tables underneath the gallery.

She arrived right after I'd plopped a huge portion of mashed potatoes on the plate.

"Don't eat it. Someone poured wine over it."

"What?"

"Some drunk idiot couldn't pour a glass and spilled the entire bottle over this table."

"Ah. All right."

"Any news?"

I told her everything. She listened, pretending to be interested in the food. We stood next to each other and whispered.

"Yes. Sophie," she said in a voice like when a mother shakes her head over her spoiled daughter. "Never mind. No harm done. Things are all right. Thanks to Simon."

"Yes. Simon always has a solution." I grinned because it was true. "He told me about his cover."

"That was brave of him. Brave and stupid. Hopefully, you'll die before someone interrogates you. And me too."

However cynical it sounded, she was right.

"Erik, I have something else for you. The SS officers act strangely. They are too happy. But no one talks about it. Even between themselves. They just grin at each other. Something must have happened. Something I must know."

My blood pressure went up. It had always meant problems for me when she spoke that way. Short sentences chopping the air and ears in a sharp voice. The urge at the end.

I tried to ease the tension. "Say no more. You want me to kill Hitler."

"That would be very useful, but no. I need you to sneak into their headquarters on Euterpestraat and figure out what the hell has happened."

Chapter 5

My head hurt, and my hands trembled. The result of drinking for a couple of nights in a row. I suffered from an unpleasant hangover. Any thoughts of booze made me want to give up and hide somewhere in the darkness and sleep for several days. Why did getting information have to lead through the glass of spirits? People had forgotten how to communicate in a normal manner. Not that I disliked having a shot or two. Even three. No problem. But pouring alcohol without limits into my body had always ended up terribly. For me. So, my head hurt, but my task had to be done. I entered the SS headquarters on Euterpestraat.

I stood in the hall, wearing an SS uniform. *Schütze* Hans Schneidler was my new identity. I'd had to drink a whole night to get this uniform. With the help of two hookers, we had gotten drunk and drugged a Nazi soldier who was about the same height as me. He had a mustache. So it should've been easy to pretend to be him and claim I had shaved the hair under my nose. The man's face changed dramatically when he shaved his mustache off, being hardly recognizable. The bloke was being held in an apartment on the north side of Amsterdam. The girls were instructed to give him more doses of sleeping pills to keep his consciousness wandering for a couple of days.

Before the Nazis had come, this building had been an elementary school. They'd made many changes here. The classrooms were split, creating many offices and inter-rogation rooms. The cellar became a prison.

A few soldiers and officers walked around, following their duties or whatever made them cross the hall. Because it was early morning, the hall wasn't crowded. Three or four people in five minutes.

Sleepy guardians were hiding in the small room, waiting for their shift to end. Everyone could see them through the window in the door. I gazed at the in-formation panel spread almost over the entire wall and had no idea where to go, what to do, and where to start. How stupid would it be to approach someone and ask why the officers had been grinning at the party?

"*Schütze!*" a voice behind my back said.

I turned. The hall was empty, except for a young Nazi officer striding toward me. He held a bunch of papers in his hand and, I didn't know why, looked pissed off. He had no SS insignias. *Wehrmacht*. What the hell was a *Wehrmacht* doing here?

"*Schütze*, what's your name?"

"Who asks?" The best way how to start a dialogue with a Nazi jerk right in their nest.

His face reddened, his shoulder moved up when he took a deep breath.

"What does this behavior mean? This is how you answer the superior officer? I am *Leutnant*, can't you see my insignia?"

"I piss on your insignia. I'm the SS, so sod off."

He stood there petrified, puffing his cheeks and his eyes out. His hands twitched. For a moment, I thought I saw him holding his breath. He represented no physical danger. I guessed he was a son of some high-ranking officer or, perhaps a son of some politician or a magnate who was sucking money from the state piggybank. I hated this type of bloke.

He swallowed. "I want you to deliver this letter to *Oberfeldarzt*, who is in city hall right now!"

To a *Wehrmacht* doctor? This would be interesting to Anna or Simon. It looked like the *Wehrmacht* was spreading its dirty fingers in Amsterdam. As if it wasn't enough that we had the SS and Gestapo here, along with NSB traitors. Hosting the army would bring the level of poverty deep down. They would eat us. Literally. And the food prices on the black market would rise astro-nomically.

"Know you what? Stick your letter right up to your arse and leave me alone. Or you will need the *artz* here and now. I'm off duty," I said in a calm voice and turned away.

The sound of a racking slide echoed in the empty hall. I turned back. The bloke held a pistol in his trembling hand. Luger P08. We locked eyes. This jerk was not able to shoot. Particularly not when no one was watching. If he had pulled the trigger, it would've been by accident, and he would have vomited even the dinner he had eaten two days ago.

I stepped closer to him. "What do you want to do with that gun, huh?"

"I'm ordering you to take this letter and deliver it to the city hall in the hands of *Oberfeldarzt*." His voice trembled, taking a higher pitch. I could sense the dryness in his throat.

My fist jerked, and the bloke bent over, letting the papers fall to the floor and pressing his hands to his nose. From between his fingers, the blood began to flow and drip right on the papers. To my surprise, he made no noise. Good. I'd had enough clamor for today. The worst brown bottle flu I had ever had.

"What the hell is going on here?!" a deep voice rumbled. An officer stood at the stairs. He'd come from upstairs, his hand still holding the railing.

"What are you two doing?!"

He darted toward us. I knew him. He was among the group of officers I'd drunk with two days ago at the NSB reception. *Hauptsturmführer* Sebastian Richter. My stomach did a few somersaults. Following Simon's advice to make acquaintances among the SS pigs, I had emptied many glasses of whiskey with him for the rest of that night, and he had talked mostly about *Herrenvolk*, the sick and twisted ideology these men had embraced. I hadn't strangled him just because Anna had cast tons of threa-tening faces every time I'd lifted my hands closer to his neck.

As he got closer, his face brightened, and he reached his hand to greet me. "*Herr* Müller! What a surprise!"

We shook hands. My first intention to be disguised as Hans Schneidler popped like a soap bubble, and I, taking the opportunity, changed my identity to Maximilian Müller again. He measured me from feet to head, shaking his head.

"What are you doing here in the SS uniform, *Herr* Müller?"

"You know, I listened carefully to what you said that night. Then I decided to join. It's my duty and my pri-vilege," I said, repeating what I'd heard almost every day from many Nazi mouths.

"Who recruited you?"

"I don't remember the names."

"Names are not like books, right?" He laughed so loud that it woke up the guardians. "To which regiment you were assigned?"

"I don't know yet."

"No problem. I will ask a few friends for a favor." He winked. "You will serve as my assistant."

"That would be a pleasure."

"And what happened here?"

I pointed my finger to the bloke who had already stood up with his hands along his body. Blood was smeared all over his face. "This *Wehrmacht* officer wanted me to do his duty and go to the city hall as a mailman."

Richter stepped closer to him and yelled to his face. "How do you dare to give orders to the SS soldier, *Leutnant?*"

The bloke shrank and babbled something I didn't understand.

"Take your papers and leave for your office, where you will wait for your commanding officer!"

The bloke went on his four and collected the papers. He stood up, saluted, raising his right hand, and clacking his heels, and strode away.

"Come, *Herr* Müller, to my office. We will have a cup of good coffee." He chuckled. "Actually, I should call you Schütze now."

He looked like he was going through an inner fight, then he waved his hand. "Never mind." The possibility of binding to him the friend of a popular officer from Berlin won. My disguise worked perfectly.

We went upstairs to his office. Richter offered me a chair, and I sat on it while he boiled the water. He prepared two cups with saucers, pouring one teaspoon of ground coffee into each. The sizzling water reached the temperature.

"So, you decided to join us?"

"Yes."

"I'm glad you did."

The coffee was good, and I enjoyed its warmth when it touched my stomach. My hangover declared retreat and backed off.

"May I ask something?" I said, pretending to be his best buddy.

"Sure, go on."

"I felt something strange since we met last time. Well, first time."

His face got confused.

"I noticed it today as well. It was like something important happened, but no one wants to talk about it."

He sighed, and his stiffened face relaxed. "For a moment, I thought you belonged to the group of men who like other men." He chuckled. "I'm happy I got it wrong."

I pretended an intense disgust. "That would never come to my mind!"

"My apologies, I didn't mean to insult you. It was just… Never mind."

"So, what is happening among us, the *Waffen-SS*?"

"Oh, that one. A great thing. We captured a British spy. Some John Smith. I don't know the details, but he will be transported to Berlin after a proper interrogation. Actually, that was the reason your friend *Obersturmführer* Herman von Dahrt came here. To start the interrogation."

"A British spy?"

"Yes. The general commanders believe they can get important information from him. The war has ended for him." He grinned. "Believe me, I wouldn't envy him. Especially, when *Obersturmführer* Herman von Dahrt is involved. He can be really cruel. Ruthless, I would say."

This would take Anna's blood pressure through the roof. A British spy captured by Nazis in the Netherlands.

Chapter 6

Hauptsturmführer Emil Hartmann Adlerstein fidgeted on the chair. It had a plain flat seat made of hardwood, and it pressed against his butt, no matter what position he was sitting in. He believed the chair had been made deliberately uncomfortable to make anyone sitting on it feel like an idiot. So that *Standartenführer* Bruno Hoffmann wouldn't feel like the only idiot in the room.

Adlerstein lifted his head and glimpsed at Hoffman, casting a light grin. He had been pretending to have an absolute interest in what Hofmann was talking about for at least the last ten minutes. Then it began to be boring. Perhaps he should fake an irresistible urge to visit a toilet. It wouldn't be faking, though. Hoffman's face made him sick.

His fingers tapped the desk in light touches, following the rhythm of the march. That was the last song he had heard when he was leaving Berlin. They had made him leave. That motherfucker *Sturmbannführer* Klaus Vogel couldn't cope with Adlerstein's presence.

He felt threa-tened. And he should be. He was a lazy idiot who couldn't even properly use cutlery. And they let him lead the squadrons. Adlerstein was way better than him. Way better than any of the high-ranking officers. And that stupid excuse. Vogel had made the decision to transfer Adlerstein to Amsterdam because, according to him, Adlerstein was too driven to serve under his command. Moron.

Only a small group of old officers had a similar military background to his. His family was ancient, and his ancestors had been great warriors, attending the biggest battles in the history of Europe. Could Vogel say something like that? Vogel? The son of a cobbler? How many boots did he have to lick to get where he was? Or Hoffman, who tried to tell something unimportant in a way as if the result of the war depended on it. Adlerstein had arrived two days ago, and the only thing he found was a mess. Complete lack of discipline. Soldiers spent the night in pubs, chasing cheap hookers, while officers got drunk every night at parties organized by the local government. How could this help him with his career? This shit hole?

"Are you listening?" Hoffman said, speaking up and interrupting Adlerstein's thoughts.

Adlerstein nodded. "Yes, of course."

"Then, please, answer my question."

Adlerstein coughed. His throat got dry. The situation wasn't getting better, and he wanted to disappear into the air forever. Away from this rotten world of bootlickers and motherfuckers. He wished he had been born in Mon-golia a thousand years ago and fought alongside Genghis Khan, the last great general.

Hoffman continued. "I received papers about you. *Sturmbannführer* Klaus Vogel wrote that you were driven and haughty."

Sturmbannführer Klaus Vogel is an idiot.

"If *Sturmbannführer* Klaus Vogel wrote it, it must be true. I can't assess myself."

Hoffman's face stiffened. It was rather funny how desperately he tried to look serious. The man who was supposed to have the whole city under his control. The imitation of the officer.

"How old are you, *Hauptsturmführer*?"

"Thirty-eight."

"Thirty-eight? You are relatively young. Look, I understand you have a hard feeling about leaving Berlin, but believe me, this place is extraordinary for an officer of your rank."

"The frontline is far away from here."

"That's true, and I like it. Drink?"

Adlerstein nodded.

Hoffman took two glasses from the tray on the small table next to his desk and filled them with the bottle he had hidden in the bottom drawer.

"I drink the Scotch. It's high quality."

Adlerstein shook his head. "*Herr Standartenführer*, I believe from the bottom of my heart that the right drink for a German soldier is the old French cognac. The older, the better. German officers drank that cognac for centuries."

"I'm sorry, but the only drink I can offer you is eighteen-year-old whisky from the highlands of Scotland," Hoffman said, handing Adlerstein the golden glass.

"*Prost!*"

Adlerstein lifted the glass. "*Prost!*"

The alcohol burned his throat. It felt to him like swallowing sandpaper. He had to fight the urge to spit it out. That would be an expression of disrespect, though. The Third Reich officer could think whatever he wanted about his superior commanding officer but never showed it.

"Good, isn't it?"

"Yes," Adlerstein said through his clenched teeth.

"This whisky is really rare to get here. Since England declared war on us, all the trade stopped." He took another sip. "Every bottle must be smuggled in, which makes the price rocket up."

"Another good reason to begin to support the cognac from France. It is our territory. You would be supporting the Third Reich."

Hoffman swallowed the last drops and put the glass on the desk.

"I like your way of thinking. You're a patriot." He poured himself another one. "But I'd rather stay with whisky. Fortunately, the money I must pay for each bottle doesn't go from my pocket."

"I don't understand, *Herr Standartenführer*."

"Look, we are going to spend some time together, and I believe you will notice it sooner or later."

He stood and began to pace the office.

"Life in Amsterdam is very convenient for many SS officers. But our pay is not the same as in Berlin. So, we need to help ourselves as much as possible. The bottles of whisky, as well as many other, I would say, treats, everything is financed from the budget I receive from the high command."

He grinned, exposing his teeth. "Who needs to change the ammunition every three months in Amsterdam? Our soldiers haven't been shooting for months. Old bullets are as good as the new ones." He sat back on his comfortable chair. "That order was just an opportunity to make business for suppliers, anyway."

That was treason. How dared he? Adlerstein decided to report this to Berlin. They should know how the officer, who should represent the Third Reich here, behaved. Perhaps this would accelerate his career. Yes, he had to obtain evidence and then arrest *Standartenführer* Bruno Hoffmann.

"Look, Emil," Hoffman said, and Adlerstein's eyes widened.

This traitor dared to call him by his name? He would show no mercy.

Hoffman nodded as if he could read Adlerstein's thoughts. "I know what you were thinking of. But I want to tell you one thing." He leaned closer." I don't care what Vogel thinks. I like to come to my own conclusions. No one will dictate to me how I should treat my officers. And I think Vogel is an idiot."

Adlerstein was surprised. He didn't expect this reaction. Not knowing what he was doing, he swallowed the rest of the whisky in his glass.

"I need someone who will be my right hand, you know? We've got a prisoner. An important prisoner. So important that *Obersturmführer* Herman von Dahrt came here to check the safety measures we took. A British spy."

Adlerstein nodded. He heard about the spy and was well aware of who *Obersturmführer* Herman von Dahrt was.

"Emil, I'm making you responsible for the prisoner's safety. He must be delivered to Berlin when von Dahrt returns. Meanwhile, it is your job to keep the prisoner safe and untouched. Do you understand?"

"*Jawohl!*"

"You will report directly to me. You will make your own decisions. I will give you a good officer from the lower ranks as your secretary and an office close to mine. You start immediately."

This was getting better and better. Hoffman's intentions were crystal clear. He wanted to get rid of responsibility, throwing everything onto Adlerstein. It might be a good opportunity, though. He imagined himself in front of the officers in Berlin. Someone mentioned Adlerstein's name and the prisoner. The important prisoner. He could form good relations with von Dahrt as well. Von Dahrt had a good reputation and was a well-recognized expert at interrogating. Perhaps trans-ferring here hadn't been so bad in the end.

"Thank you, *Herr Standartenführer.*"

"Bruno."

"Thank you, Bruno."

Chapter 7

All eyes pierced through me with daggers. I stepped into the coffee house wearing the Nazi uniform. That was a sin, and it was me who committed that sin, although the circumstances required it. All lips muted. All words disappeared in the air. Like waving a magical wand, coffee cups and small plates with French cakes became points of highest interest for everyone inside. I nodded at a known face, following the habit of greeting people, but she turned away from me. *No coffee for me today here.*

I spotted Anna sitting in the shady corner. Her red jacket contrasted with everything around her like a lighthouse. She found a good spot, nobody occupying the surrounding tables. Suitable for some serious talk. On the table was a cup of coffee and an empty plate with a few brown crumbs—the remains of the chocolate cake she had eaten. I didn't know she had a sweet tooth.

"Hey, Anna."

"Erik!" She covered her mouth, filtering the laughter through her fingers. "You look…strange."

"Well, I didn't want this. Do you remember?"

"Sure I do. Still, though. It's fun to see you wearing that uniform." Her shoulders wobbled, and then she burst into subdued laughter.

I put my hand on the chair's back and waited for her to regain her stoic calm. I must have looked like a clown because there was only a tiny group of things in this world that could make her laugh. She smiled often, though, that was part of the game she played.

The silence deepened. People sitting behind us at tables arranged in two rows gazed at us, waiting for what would happen next. Even the waiters at the counter stopped polishing the glasses and cups. The cozy room, full of coffee smell, got darker when I sat on the chair.

I gazed at them and said loudly enough: "What?!"

Everybody tilted their heads and continued eating cakes or drinking whatever had been served to them.

"I'm sorry, Erik. I couldn't help myself. No offense," Anna said, chuckling between words.

"None taken. Just, please, don't tell anyone. I have some reputation, you know?"

"No worries." She yanked the hem of her red jacket down and smoothed it with her hand. That serious face I had known her for returned.

"Enough jokes," she said, swallowing the remains of the chuckler. "People are staring at us. What do you have?"

I gazed around, and when I was sure nobody was listening, I leaned closer. "They got a British spy," I whispered and straightened my back.

"A British spy?"

I nodded. She processed the information for a while.

"All right. Start with his name. Do you know it?"

"His name is John Smith."

"John Smith?! Are you sure?"

"Yes."

"Did you see papers with his name written down?"

I shook my head. "No. I got this information from the SS officer."

"Did you see him?"

"No. That would be too risky. He's guarded better than the virginity of a noble family's daughter."

She stopped listening and rummaged through her purse. Finding what she was looking for, she put a small cigarette case on the table. The lighter followed, and Anna lit her indispensable cigarette, blowing the smoke above our heads. A definite sign she was diving into deep thinking.

"That name doesn't sound familiar. On the contrary, it is more than a common name in Great Britain," she said after making a couple of gray-blue clouds.

"I hope you didn't expect King George."

"No. But anyway, it doesn't ring any bells."

"Do you know the names of all British spies in the Secret Intelligence Service?"

"Of course not. And it's not SIS anymore. They call it MI6 now. Go on, tell me more."

I told her everything I had. *Hauptsturmführer* Sebastian Richter had spilled all the beans he'd been aware of. The guards in the corridor and the guards behind the iron doors made of steel rods. Random guard changes kept all officers and soldiers on edge, everyone in the highest state of readiness, forgoing nightly pleasures. I didn't forget to mention the *Wehrmacht* settling in Amsterdam.

She listened, all ears, puffing the cigarette and sipping coffee. Then, Anna fell into her deepest thoughts. I'd been suspecting she was involved in international operations. The information about a foreign citizen, a member of a secret agency, being kept in the Netherlands must have been stabbing needles into her mind.

I took another look around, seeking someone who would make me a cup of coffee or, at least, bring me a glass of water or lemonade. No one cared, though. The Nazi uniform became uncomfortable, itching on my skin. My mind could focus only on taking a shower and resting for a while. Like a week or so.

Anna lifted her head and lit another cigarette. That made me sad. If the war and the occupation didn't kill her, the cigarettes would.

"Erik, we need to free the spy," she said.

I shook my head. "Impossible."

"Try harder. You're not known for saying the 'impossible' word."

"Good move, Anna. Normally, it would motivate me. But the answer is still 'not possible'."

"Listen, Erik, you have the skills to get past the guards without being noticed. Your goal would be to reach the area where the prisoner is held. Once there, find a way to unlock all the doors. And you can use that new friend of yours."

I sighed. "No. Having acquaintances among the SS officers is fine but also limiting." I told her about the post *Hauptsturmführer* Sebastian Richter had offered me.

Her eyes widened. "That's awesome. You are going to be right where the things are happening!"

"Not exactly. Richter's responsibilities are nothing important. He coordinates with the local gendarmerie. He has no access to the prisoner. The prison is commanded by some Adlerstein."

"Adlerstein?"

"Have you heard about him?"

She nodded, and I waited till her thoughts were organized again.

"Yes. He's new here. I haven't met him yet, but I heard about him. A strange man. Dangerous, though. He even refused the invitation to the party organized by the mayor."

"The one I was at?"

"No. Before that."

"I will mention this to Simon. Perhaps he can come up with something."

I shook my head again. "I'm afraid he'll tell you the same. Don't push on it, Anna, please. Many people would die if the resistance tried it." I gazed around for the third time. "I want a coffee."

"I understand the danger, don't worry," Anna said. "It just tickles me. Getting a favor from the British MI6… That would be priceless."

Her mind went for another trip to the abyss of her inner universe while her hands automatically reached for the cup. She put the empty cup to her lips, trying to sip the already-drunk coffee. That kicked her back to reality. She lifted the cup, attracting the attention of the old waiter, who stood behind the counter and polished the glasses for serving the lemonade.

The waiter approached, took the empty cup, and put it on the plate with cake crumbs.

"Would you make me another coffee, please? And one for this young gentleman," she said.

The waiter stiffened, casting a face full of disgust. He said nothing, just stared at her as if she said something in a language he didn't understand. After a while, he turned away.

"Walter, wait!" Her voice hit him hard, resonating in the small space.

He stopped but didn't turn at her.

"Walter, I asked you for a coffee."

He couldn't resist and stepped closer. "How could you, Anna? I have known you since you were a child, and now, this?"

Anna's face hardened. Each cell on her facial skin yelled. Her eyes were in the flames, burning anyone who would resist.

"This is what you think about me?!"

Beads of sweat developed on the waiter's forehead. The rattling of the cup on the plate revealed that his hand was trembling.

"Walter, I would never do anything like that, and you know it."

The waiter opened his mouth, but Anna interrupted him. "Don't ask any questions!" Like a whip.

The waiter shrank.

"Please, bring us two cups of coffee and a glass of water for this young man." Her voice changed. It was a voice people were using to talk to their closest friends. Warm. That was the only word I could think of.

The waiter nodded, casting a shy grin at us, and returned to the counter. In a few seconds, steam sizzled from the coffee maker.

"And old family friend," Anna said.

"I see you have a good relationship."

"Let it be, Erik. I need to think."

I got my coffee and a glass of water. It came right in time. Otherwise, I would melt away. Anna kept her silence, so I enjoyed the refreshments. I didn't intend to stay for a long time. The longer it took, the less comfortable I felt wearing the Nazi uniform. I thanked her for the coffee and left, offering my hand to the waiter before stepping out on the street. He shook it.

My path back to the pub where the girls kept drunk and drugged Hans Schneidler led around the SS headquarters block on Euterpestraat. The street was quiet. Something was wrong, though. I looked closer. The wall of the old school moved out and returned as if the building was breathing. Hallucinations? Deprivation of sleep or some strange post-hangover? The answer came right after. The wall moved again, this time followed by fire, smoke, and dust. A loud explosion. The sound wave deafened my ears, leaving only the hum of my own blood.

Someone had set a bomb inside the SS headquarters, and it went off.

Chapter 8

I ran toward the entrance, jumping like a hunted deer trying to escape. The dust from bricks mixed with smoke created a cloud hanging just above the street. Who could have done this? Who was so stupid to set a bomb in the SS headquarters? The consequences would be fatal for Amsterdam. For us. The images of the near future flashed through my mind. None of them pleased me.

People from nearby buildings gathered in front of the building. Faces stuck out of the windows. Everyone was hungry for information about what happened, so later, they would spread gossip. I tried to push through the crowd, but it was impossible without using force. My ears were still humming, and I wasn't in the mood for that. Gazing over the people's heads, I saw the plaster coming off the wall on the first and second floors.

I grabbed the nearest bloke by the sleeve and turned him. "What happened?"

It happened to be the low-ranking SS officer. "A bomb went off," he said, satisfying his urge to explain the obvious.

He wasn't helping. However, the stupid question required a stupid answer.

I grabbed him again. "Did someone die?"

"I don't know. Let me be, *Schütze!*" he said and jerked off my grip.

I took a deep breath and lowered my hand, forgotten in the air. I had to know what had happened and how. I had to know if someone had been killed. Leaning forward to get at the level of people's waists, I rocketed toward the place of the explosion, making a path with my elbows. After eight or ten feet, I spotted the damaged wall. Although, damaged was a too strong word for this. Whoever had done this, he'd done it wrong. I expected a massive hole in the wall and dead bodies lying on the shattered bricks and plaster. Nothing like that. They must have used the gunpowder trapped in some metallic vessel. Not dynamite or other explosives. The plaster fell off the wall. That was the only damage the explosion did. And broken windows in some rooms in the basement.

Two bodies were lying on the dusty ground. Two alive bodies. Blokes waved their hands. One hand bled. I believed they had been close when the bomb went off. A group of soldiers brought stretchers and put the bodies on them. Armed guards kept the observing watchers aside.

The action without effect. Worse, though. The action that would endanger us, the citizens. The question returned to my mind. Who? It wasn't Simon and his blokes. I knew them. They would've blasted half of the building into the air. It must have been someone who had been forced to operate quickly without securing the results. Someone not from this city. Someone who didn't know us and what we were doing. The British. This idea scared me. The foreign service, the number one enemy of our occupants, operated on our land. That was not possible without the help from the locals. The SS would go crazy. So would the Gestapo. Göring's monkeys kept a small group of agents here, competing with the SS. They would hit the underground, and it would be hard. I had to do something.

Hauptsturmführer Adlerstein stood by the window, observing the chaos on the street. The explosion had broken his thoughts. Something unexpected. A tactical move from the enemies. Incredibly stupid, though. It was apparent that installing a bomb into the building from the street would've done no harm. It had exploded toward outside. Yet somebody had done it, targeting the pri-soner. His prisoner. Who could've been so childishly naïve?

This wasn't an operation performed by the local resistance. Adlerstein believed there was one in

Amsterdam. Everywhere was at least one group of people hoping that they could stand against the strength of the Third Reich. Like children believing in fairy tales. No one could. Their activities stung unpleasantly, though, often by killing innocent soldiers who could have fought on the front lines.

The way the bomb was set pointed to someone outside Amsterdam. He believed it had been the British. They had tried to kill the agent, preventing him from speaking. Too late. They didn't know that he, Adlerstein, was here, taking care of the prisoner. How could they even get here? That was the unavoidable result of loose discipline among the SS troops and officers. *Standartenführer* Bruno Hoffmann had no idea how to command and lead. When this was over, Adlerstein would take his place and establish order.

The phone rang. He turned away from the window and gazed at it, reluctant to pick up the handset. Whoever that might be, this was the worst time for phone calls. After several rings, he leaned over the desk, reaching with his hand.

"Adlerstein?" Hoffman's voice sounded nervous.

"Yes."

"Did you notice what happened?"

"Yes, I did."

"Do you think the same thing as I do?"

Moron! As if I could read his thoughts. "I'm afraid I don't."

"This has to stop now, Adlerstein! I don't want any bomb attacks here. Especially not from the British!"

Hoffman's last words surprised him. That stupid bag of potatoes had got it right!

"Do something with it. Catch people who did it or whatever," Hoffman continued.

"I'm preparing the plan for strengthening the security in the prison."

"That won't help. We need to get all those criminals and hang them to warn the others."

"That would be impossible…"

"I made YOU responsible for the prisoner, as far as I can remember. Do whatever you need to do. You have until this evening. Do you understand?"

"*Jawohl!*"

"And, Adlerstein."

"Yes."

"Never ever tell me that something is not possible!" Hoffman hung up.

Adlerstein returned to the window. The dust cloud had already fallen to the ground or blown away. More and more people came to see what happened. Catching the culprits was out of the question. They were either far away from Amsterdam or already dead, committing sui-cide. In a strange way, Hoffman had been right. He had to warn the other criminals. But not by chasing the wind on the field.

He went to the door and opened it.

"Klaus!"

His assistant jumped from the window, where he watched the street as well. "*Jawohl! Herr Hauptsturmführer!*"

"Listen carefully to what you are going to do!" Klaus sat down in a chair and prepared a piece of paper and a pen.

"Prepare an order for *Hauptsturmführer* Richter to find all prisoners suspected of being local resistance members. He will interrogate them if they know something about this attack."

The pen stopped, and Klaus gazed at Adlerstein, waiting for more instructions.

"After interrogating them, he will hang them all, and you, Klaus, you will make sure the local underground knows about it. Do you understand?"

"*Jawohl! Herr Hauptsturmführer!*"

"Start now!"

"*Jawohl! Herr Hauptsturmführer!*"

Adlerstein returned to his office, closing the door behind him. Klaus looked like a responsible person. This first serious task would test him if he could be trusted. But first, the most important thing. He picked up the headset and spun the hand crank.

"Operator," the voice said.

"Connect me with the train station!"

"*Jawohl!*"

Waiting, Adlerstein put his thoughts together. This was a brilliant idea. He would protect the prisoner and, at the same time, protect the SS headquarters from any fur-ther attacks. That moron Hoffman had no idea who the prisoner really was. How precious he was. Precious because the prisoner would help Adlerstein to move higher in the *Wehrmacht*.

"*Stationschef* Beenhouwer," the voice said in Dutch.

"*Sprachen Sie Deutsch?* Do you speak German?"

"Yes."

"This is *Hauptsturmführer* Adlerstein. When is the next train to Berlin?"

"In fifty minutes the regular express train leaves the station."

"It will have a new passenger. Now, listen carefully. I need you to change the train and add some more cars."

"That's impossible. The train has already been pre-pared and is waiting to leave the station."

"Do you want me to come there personally and explain what is possible and what isn't?!"

Adlerstein heard the man on the other end swal-lowing. It went hard down his throat.

"No," he said in a low voice after a while.

"Listen carefully to what I'm going to dictate!"

"Yes, *Herr Hauptsturmführer!*"

The cloud dissolved, and more people came to watch the extraordinary scene. This would keep people busy for weeks.

A known face appeared at the entrance to the building. My new boss, *Hauptsturmführer* Richter. I took a step toward him, but hands holding a submachine gun pressed against my chest. The soldier, a young man, gazed at me. His face prayed for me not to move further, not to make a problem for him. This child wouldn't survive a minute in a perilous situation. Blokes like him were always those who died first, showing to others what not to do.

"I'm the assistant of *Hauptsturmführer* Sebastian Richter," I said in a calm voice.

The pressure weakened. He furrowed his eyebrows as if he was reading my mind. Then he released his hands and let me go.

Richter was busy giving orders to soldiers and organizing everything. I touched his arm, and he startled.

"Oh, Max." He grinned. "I almost shit my pants when it exploded."

"We need to talk."

"Just a second," he said and turned to some officer. "Tell the guards commander to scatter these people!"

The officer saluted, clacking his heels, and left. Richter returned his face to me and sighed.

"Hard times, my friend. This shouldn't have happened. I got orders to operate in emergency mode."

"Emergency mode?"

"Yes, I can't leave the headquarters for the next two or three days."

"What does it mean?"

He shrugged. "No party for me tonight."

"Oh, I thought you were going to shoot someone or something like that."

"No, not me. I had to order the gendarmerie to gather people from the local underground and all the prisoners we had in jail. And the worst, I must interrogate them personally."

"Why do you need to do that?"

"My commander believes someone helped the British to set the bomb here."

I swallowed.

He noticed it and nodded. His voice got a sad subtone. "Yes. And that's not all. That new jerk, *Hauptsturmführer* Adlerstein, wants me to hang all prisoners."

"Hang them? Why?"

"I don't know. But I don't like it. Why hang those people? We depend on them."

"What?!"

"Yes, we do. It sounds strange, but the fact is we could wipe out the underground in one night. Just a short call to Berlin, and they would send thousands of troops. That would be a massacre. Something similar to what happened to the Temple Knights."

He nodded again.

"And why you don't want to do that?" I said.

He chuckled and took my arm. We walked away from the entrance. The soldiers were pushing the people far-ther from the destroyed place. One idiot hit an innocent man trying to pass through the crowd.

"Because then, then would be no point for us staying here," Richter whispered. "No underground, no need for the SS. Berlin is fine, believe me. But I don't want to go back. Amsterdam suits me better. And not just me."

He winked and went to organize the soldiers, shouting at the soldier who was too proactive. I knew what was hiding behind Richter's words. In Berlin, he was no one. Here, he was king and lived a satisfying life full of nights of drinks and hookers for free.

Interrogating the underground was dangerous to everyone. Someone would spill the beans, that was for sure. The SS methods could make a cold stone speak. I stepped toward him again.

"Sebastian!"

He gazed around, and when he realized it was me, he put his finger on his lips, the fear reflecting from his face.

"Shhh, Max. Call me *Herr Hauptsturmführer* when on duty, all right?"

I nodded and leaned closer to his head.

"You can save your position in Amsterdam."

"How?"

"Who will check whether you hung those people?"

He tilted his head, casting questions from his eyes.

"No, really. Tell me, who will check and count the dead bodies?"

His face brightened with understanding, smoothing wrinkles under his eyes.

"No one," he whispered.

"Exactly! You know what I mean."

He nodded.

"You don't need to hang anyone."

He nodded.

"You will stay here forever."

Richter leaned back, whispering to my ears. "You're a good assistant, Max."

"I know."

"I will finish organizing the prisoner's transport, and we can go for lunch together."

He winked again and left toward another group of soldiers, who were trying to sweep the mess of shattered plaster with brooms. I grabbed his sleeve.

"What transport?!"

"The British spy. Adlerstein is sending him to Berlin by train. On the civil train, would you believe? I have to organize the transport to the train station with the local gendarmerie."

Now things took on a different glitter. Some things began to make sense. That man, who was lying on the bed in the basement, wasn't *just* a spy. He was an important spy. Otherwise, the SS wouldn't protect him by sending him away after a failed sabotage attempt. Anna wanted to get a favor from the British. Nonsense. I couldn't resist the feeling that the game was more complicated. I had to go with him and check on him. Or free him. Or kill him if necessary. It would be extremely dangerous, though, and I might end up dead.

"Everything all right?" a sudden voice said. I startled. Thomas! The troop from the resistance. I knew him well. He was close to Simon.

"What the hell are you doing here?" I said and began to stroll toward the entrance.

"I was around when it happened. What are you doing here in that uniform?" He followed me, keeping a distance sufficient for talking.

The sun jumped over the roof of the building. I stopped and squinted into it. The sun beams caressed my face. The warmth was convenient. I turned to Thomas.

"I'm all right. And happy you're here. Please, go and tell Simon to follow the train to Berlin. I'm going with the squad and will try to free the British spy. I need him to pick us up when we jump off the train."

He looked surprised.

"Tell him that the SS are going to interrogate the underground because of the explosion. Some people may be hung, but I did my best to prevent it."

I spun on my feet and headed back, following Richter.

Chapter 9

The seam on the trousers pressed against my skin, leaving inconvenient itching. More and more I hated to wear this uniform. The empty car rattled. Almost all seats were unmounted except the two rows at the opposite end. The partitions separating the vestibule in the middle from the seat sections were disassembled, creating a space from gangway to gangway. I was on duty with Stefan Fischer, the man with the saddest eyes I had ever seen, sitting on the cold, dirty floor. He sat next to me, leaning back against the wall. We guarded the entrance to the rear gangway of the prison car. I should stand, but I didn't give a shit. I was tired. Tired of this uniform. Tired of people I had to call 'my squad' and of raising my hand whenever some dumb officer flashed his ugly face around. Not the dream I would've wished for. I fit in, though, and that mattered.

I'd convinced Richter to help me to join the guards and send me on the train. He had been reluctant, but I promised him I would ask *Obersturmführer* Herman von

Dahrt to be his close friend when I came back. He believed this lie. The train had left Amsterdam at eleven sharp. *Hauptsturmführer* Emil Hartmann Adlerstein, the Nazi officer responsible for the prisoner's safety, must have made bloody hell for the railroad workers. Those poor blokes had used some special magic and reshuffled the train cars, adding a few more and alternating their interiors. All in time. That deserved respect. Respect they would never get from these stupid Nazi heads.

I forced myself to focus on my task, ignoring everything around me. I knew they kept the spy right in the prison car guarded by two other men. Two squads looked after the entrances to the gangways in the empty passenger cars before and after the prison car, rotating the guards every two hours. More soldiers waited off duty in the next car behind us. Off duty but ready to jump and fire. Adlerstein had come up with a clever solution. Even if anyone passed the soldiers at the gangway, two more MP40s would wait for him inside. Although, his plan was lacking ingenuity because, when off duty, I would be able to pace through the entire train without drawing attention. That was my first advantage. Adlerstein didn't know I was there. That was my second advantage. Life had taught me that every solution had at least one weakness. But for now, I had no clue what the weakness was. That kicked all my advantages right to the arse, sending them straight to hell, and I was at the beginning—I knew many facts, but they were worthless.

"What did you do before the war?" Stefan said, knocking me out of my thoughts.

"What?"

"What did you do before the war? I was a teacher."

"A teacher? I was a student."

"What did you study?"

"The psychology and physiology of the street gangs."

His face reddened, and his lost-in-the-forest-calf eyes went deeper into sadness. Stefan spun his head toward the window, observing the country flowing around. He raised his finger and counted the trees.

I had no idea how long distance the train had gone so far nor how many miles remained to Berlin. The final destination didn't sound delightful to my ears. I expected a welcoming committee of dozens of Nazis armed to the teeth, ready to empty their mags. The rescue had to be done as soon as possible. The main guards inside didn't bother me. Two shots; problem solved. But what then? Jump out? The railroad was far from perfect, so the train had to slow down. A child on a bicycle could have gone faster. A jump sounded like a solution, but it had to be done immediately after killing the guards. Hopefully the terrain lacked trees and rocks. If not, we would have to wait for the next opportunity to jump, and the soldiers in the guard cars might step in, lured by the noise from shooting or by the signalization installed from car to car. I couldn't handle bullets from two opposing directions. If long-lasting bindings had incapacitated the spy, that would be the same. Just sit and wait for him to get better. The risk indicator rocketed upward. I had to see the prisoner before I planned anything.

"I taught history. On *Gymnasium*," Stefan said.

I gazed at him. A chatty bloke. I let it go on.

"*Gymnasium?*"

"The secondary school in Germany. We prepared students for universities offering a more academically oriented education."

"I know what *Gymnasium* is. The Netherlands has *Gymnasiums*, too," I said. "Middle-class students?"

"Yes. Mostly."

"Did you like it?"

"I would say endlessly."

"Then, why did you leave?"

Stefan shrugged and continued counting the trees passing by.

I pulled the sleeve of his jacket. "Hey, I mean it. Why did you leave?"

He cast his sad eyes at me, and I knew immediately this man had gone through a life tragedy. His body shrank, pulling his head deeper between his shoulders. That triggered my curiosity. What story was hiding behind that innocent face?

"I don't think I want to talk about it," he said, tilting his head against the wall.

"All right, I understand. Tell me why you don't want to talk about it?"

A dramatic pause followed by more trees counting. This time, without pointing a finger.

"I don't know you," he said after a while.

"That's correct. I don't know you either. That doesn't mean we can't share stories, though. We are going to spend some time together, you know?"

He sighed. "You aren't from Germany, right?"

"I was born in the Netherlands."

"Then you won't understand."

"Understand what?"

"The way we live." He paused. "The way we have to live."

"Is it different from the rest of the world? Don't you breathe the air? Or you eat grass and shit golden eggs?"

He sighed again. I spotted the inner battle he was fighting. He put his hands on his bent knees and stared at his fingers, playing with them on the invisible piano. I let him breathe. He would continue when he needed to.

"It's the government, you know?"

"You mean Hitler?"

He jerked his head and gazed around as if he was checking if there was somebody who could listen. The habit.

"Yes, Hitler. Look, it can't be compared. I've been in Amsterdam for a while, and it's different."

"What is different."

"How to... All right, you can speak freely without fear of being arrested."

"You think so?"

"Yes. I do. The SS and the Gestapo have ears everywhere. In Amsterdam, there are only a few SS soldiers. No stool pigeons."

"Well, that's not true. We don't have the SS as strong as in Germany, but we have our own stool pigeons who tip the authorities off. Perhaps it is worse because those stool pigeons make quite a good living out of it."

"But, did people disappear? Just because they said something wrong?"

"You would be surprised. Thousands of them. You must understand. Our gendarmerie does the same as *Sicherheitspolizei* does in Germany. In Amsterdam, they call it 'hunting the inner enemy'."

He tilted his head and dropped down his shoulders. His bubble burst, but I didn't feel like a winner. Why did he think that it was different in other countries? Of course, it wasn't.

"But your countries didn't experience raids of the SA members."

"Stefan, we are not comparing willies here. Or who had worse suffering. That's out of the question. The regime is bad and rots. And people suffer everywhere under it. That's what is happening."

He grinned. "You don't speak like the others do."

"Why should I?"

"The government spreads fear among the people. They do it intentionally. It's easier to be feared than loved, you know?"

I was amazed. Where had I heard that before?

"Yes, I know. So, that's why you left teaching?"

Stefan nodded, still staring at his fingers.

"Did they threaten you?"

"Yes. Can be said that way. I left by myself. I didn't want to teach twisted history. The *Reichserziehungsministerium,* the Reich Education Ministry dictates everything taught. They told me if I hadn't taught what they dictated, I would be banned from teaching. So, I left."

"Yes, to the SS." I tapped him on his shoulder, grinning. "Good move."

"It was the only option I had after leaving *Gymnasium.* To serve in the army or go to the camp. They would have destroyed me and my relatives if I had refused. Fortunately, I got to Amsterdam thanks to my uncle, who knows somebody in the high command. But it cost a lot of money."

He sighed again. Too much for me to cope with. His fingers waved in the air. The silence was heavy, and we consumed all of the oxygen in the closed space of the train car. Perhaps he hated the regime, but he did what the others did. A little bit of hypocrisy, right? I moved my focus to the window. Outside, the country ran along the train in the opposite direction. The sun was almost touching the zenith. Time flew, and I, instead of doing something useful, I was thinking about how sad the story of this 30-year-old man was. *Stop being silly and focus on what's important, Erik.*

How could I get closer to the prisoner without them killing me in an instant?

"Why did you join the SS?" His voice tore my thoughts apart.

"What?!"

"Why did you…"

"I know what you asked. It just surprised me. All right, I would say I wanted to save as many lives as possible by not shooting when shooting was required."

"I'm not getting it. If you didn't want to shoot, you shouldn't have joined the SS."

"No, quite the opposite. They want me to shoot, but I refuse. And that saves lives."

"Did you shoot at someone?"

"No, not since I've worn the SS uniform."

"*Unterscharführer* will shoot you the first time you refuse the order."

"No, he won't. I will kill him first."

He laughed. That was catchy, and I laughed with him.

Then his face got the same sad cover as a few minutes ago, and he tilted his head down. "I can't shoot, and I pray not to get into a situation where I will have to."

The seconds passed by. Stefan lifted his head and grinned at me. "I like you, Max. You're different."

"You bet I am."

"I think I can talk about anything with you. Like, you wouldn't tell anyone about this, right?"

"That's a bit naïve to ask me that favor, but don't worry. You're right. I won't tell anyone."

"Even if you were in danger?"

"Even then."

"Even before Hitler."

"Hitler is a piece of shit, Stefan. You should be aware of it, after all."

That made him open his mouth wide while releasing a long sigh. "I don't like the government, but I have never said things like that," he said after a lengthy processing period.

"It's simple. Just take a deep breath and say, 'Hitler is a moron'."

"No, I don't want to say it." His head was shaking vigorously.

"Come on, Stefan. That's freedom. The freedom they have taken from us. Freedom. Can you feel it?" I said, not knowing why. Something bothered me and made me tease him. Although, I felt stupid doing it. But I couldn't resist.

"No!"

"Say 'Hitler is a moron'." I pulled his arm, turning him toward me.

He jerked off my grip, covering his ears with his palms and curling up in a ball. I stood and grabbed him by the uniform.

"Say it, Stefan!"

He nodded, keeping his palms on his ears. I could hear him laughing.

"No! I will not say 'Hitler is a moron'!"

"You have just said that!"

"No! I haven't!"

The train suddenly stopped as if someone had pulled the emergency brake. The inertia was too strong, and I fell on the floor next to Stefan. He looked scared.

"Listen!" he said.

The roar of an engine rumbled through the window. It was far away from us, but was getting closer.

"What's that?"

I shrugged. "I don't know. A plane, perhaps."

We sprang from the floor and glued our faces against the window glass, gazing at the nearby green hill and squinting our eyes against the blue sky. The roar got stronger.

A shadow crossed the shade of the car interior. Spitfire!

Chapter 10

"What is this?" Stefan said.

"It's a plane."

"I know that it's not a flying pig. Whose plane is it? Ours?"

"No. It's a Spitfire. Check the military insignia. Blue, white, and red in a circle. Does it look German?"

"No."

"Do Germans fly Spitfires?"

"No, they don't."

"Of course, they don't. The plane is British."

He gazed at me, shaking his head. "What would a British plane do here?"

That was a good question. Fighting pilots always flew in couples. A single plane deep inside the enemy territory could be either spying or on a secret mission.

"I have no idea," I said.

Spitfire flew over the train in the opposite direction. We jumped at the window across the aisle and observed it. The pilot climbed a bit and turned the plane, facing the train again. The maneuver looked awkward, as if the plane was too heavy to do that. It didn't make sense. I'd seen the demonstration of *Luchtvaartbrigade*, the Dutch Air Force, and they turned the planes way easily.

The plane approached, and the pilot began to fire. The flashes reveal the position of its machine guns. Two. Not four, not eight. Two only. Why? The pilot targeted the middle of the train. Why?

"He's coming after us!" Stefan said and crouched, covering his head with his palms.

"Don't panic. We are not in the firing line."

He raised his head, watching through the window. "You're right," he said and stood up.

Getting closer to the train, the plane began to climb again. When it lifted its nose, I spotted two bombs mounted under the wings. Bombs? I'd heard that Spitfires could carry bombs, but why here in this situation? A British plane in the air armed with two bombs and a British spy kept in the prison on the train wasn't a coincidence. No. I didn't believe it was.

Stefan had similar thoughts. "I guess he wants to free the spy," he said.

I doubted it. How would the pilot get the spy into the plane? No, there must have been something else. He was preparing the battlefield. The second attack would be on the ground. I opened the window and looked around, carefully scanning the surroundings, but I couldn't see anything. No trucks, no people, nothing. I opened the window and stuck my head out. I could spot the last car as it was behind the slight turn. The muzzle flashes from the machine guns glimmered in the shadows of the open box car. The Nazis returned the fire, aiming at the plane.

"I can't see it. Where is it?" Stefan said, sticking his head through the opposite window.

"On this side," I said.

He walked to the middle of the train car and gazed out. "I can see it from here. He's getting low again."

I tried to focus. If the British used the plane to incapacitate the train security, why did the pilot shoot in the middle of the train? The danger came from the last car with the machine guns. Only if his target weren't the soldiers.

"He's shooting again!" Stefan's voice came to me from the distance.

"What?"

He turned his face at me. "He's shooting again."

"Oh. I think he will attack a few more times."

The roar approached and flew over the train. Stefan changed sides, gazing through another window. He was like a child who was seeing a plane for the first time. I watch the plane taking another turn and shooting. The same direction again. Then I got it. The pilot wasn't preparing the battlefield. There was no battlefield. He wanted to kill the spy. He wanted to mute him forever. A sacrifice the British were willing to make.

I peered through the small window on the gangway door but couldn't see inside the prison car. From here, it looked like it was not damaged. I had to go there and check.

The pilot led the plane to another attack. I stiffened for a moment. This time, our car was the target. The small dust clouds on the ground left by the bullets revealed the direction. I gazed at Stefan. He stood right in the firing line. A crazy bloke was petrified, pointing his finger through the window. The dusty clouds were getting closer and closer.

I ran and bumped into him, throwing him off. He fell on the floor, and I fell next to him. The bullets from the .303 machine gun pierced the wooden car wall, as well as the floor. Right where Stefan had stood a half a second before. He lay on his back, his face pale. The plane roared behind the hill.

"That was…"

"Next time, check the bullet traces on the ground. They will show you where the pilot is going to shoot," I said and stood up.

The train jerked and began to move again.

Stefan kept the lying position. I stuck out from the window. The plane became a dark spot painted in the sky way behind the train, but it approached fast. Something was different. The pilot dived the plane in one straight line. This wasn't a position for shooting. He was going to drop a bomb.

My muscles twitched. The urge to jump off the train was strong. Dropping a bomb would cause fatal damage to the car I was in. If the pilot hit the target. He could have missed, and the bomb would have fallen far away from the train. If I jumped and he missed, I would never get back on the train. What to do?

I stepped to the door in the middle of the car and coped with the thought of jumping off the train. Outside, a field of green stems filled the view. Probably corn. Didn't matter. Grabbing the door handle, I yanked the door open and put one foot on the first step. Flowing air hit my face and welled my eyes with tears. The plane loomed over me. Its engine pitch whining higher from the increasing speed.

"What are you doing?!" Stefan said.

I gazed at him. He stood next to me, shocked, questions in his eyes. I didn't know what was happening inside me, but I grabbed his forearm.

"Be ready to jump!"

"Why?!"

"Look!" I leaned back, making space for him to gaze in the plane's direction. He stuck his head out and jerked himself back, shaking his head.

"We have to jump!" I said, fighting with the noise from the racing train.

"Why?!"

"Didn't you see what the plane is up to?!"

He shook his head.

"It's going to drop the bomb on us!"

He poked his head out again, glancing at the plane's direction. Then he gazed at me. His face was too close to mine to see what was happening behind him. His contours hazed. At the upper left corner of his eyes, I spotted a fire blast. The sound wave reached us despite the train running away from it. It was loud. Stefan covered his head with his hands and hunched.

The Nazis shot the plane down. Right before it could drop the bomb. They must have been lucky or had a canon I didn't know about. It was hard to take down the plane, even with a fast-firing MG42. Nevertheless, the plane exploded, and the pilot died. End of story.

Stefan returned inside, and I followed, closing the door with mixed feelings. I was still alive. The spy was still in captivity, most likely alive. Nothing had changed; only one life had ended. A pure example of futility.

"Does it mean we don't need to jump?"

I nodded, saying nothing. He must have sensed my thoughts because he sat on the floor and backed off from any questions.

The gangway door opened, and an *Unterscharführer* who commanded the squad to which I was assigned to entered, wobbling with the rhythm of the train shocks when strolling from the prison car.

"Are you all right here?" he said.

Stefan stood from the floor. "Yes."

"No one's hurt?"

"No one."

He chuckled. "It was hell, wasn't it? Fucking plane with the fucking British pilot."

"Did he get the prisoner?" I said.

"No. He couldn't. But that fucker got Dietrich. He drilled the holes through his entire body. Good that our gunners blew him off." He gazed around. "You will be changed soon. Wait here!"

He strolled toward the other end of the train car and suddenly turned back to us. "And don't sit on the floor. Otherwise, I will run you to court martial!" And he left.

I was right in my guess. The prisoner remained untouched after all. My role here hadn't ended. Any way I looked at it, it didn't make me happy.

Stefan stood like a statue, gazing at me.

"What?" I said.

"Thank you," he said in a low voice. "Thank you very much. You saved my life, and I will never forget that."

Chapter 11

Hauptsturmführer Adlerstein closed the door of the box car with the machine guns and stood on the gangway, squinting into the sun. The sky was clear, and no plane was floating in the blue space. No enemy's plane. Spotting a Messerschmitt would be welcome. The air stream cooled down his body, making him shiver despite the warmth from the sun. The gangway rocked under his feet. The state of the railroad was horrible. He held the railings with one hand and stepped forward. The state had no money to fix everything. *Führer* had no money. He needed it for a higher purpose than fixing railroads in subordinate countries. Adlerstein entered the passenger car.

The car's vestibule was dark, and the air inside smelled of fecal from the toilet. Adlerstein strode across. He had to check on the prisoner and gather all his officers. The attack proved his idea of installing four machine guns had been effective. It reduced the supply of ammunition to less than half, though. They might not survive a second attack. If there is to be a second attack. He had to be prepared for all possible options. Hopes wouldn't help. And he had to change the plan. The enemy wouldn't ex-pect that. Adlerstein opened the door to the aisle.

"You! *Schütze*! Come here!"

The soldier sitting on the seat next to the door jumped on his feet and saluted, clacking his feet. "*Jawohl!*"

"Run through the train and tell all the officers to gather in my coupe!"

"*Jawohl!*" The heels of the heavy military boots clacked again, and the soldiers rocketed toward the last car.

"Halt!"

The soldier stopped, freezing all movements, and gazed at Adlerstein. His face impassive, expressing no emotions.

"Except *Untersturmführer* Klein, do you understand?!"

"*Jawohl!*" The soldier turned on his heel and ran in the opposite direction.

Adlerstein observed him as he leaped between the passengers who stood or strolled the aisle. A good soldier. No questions, no doubts. Jumping and following orders. He tried to remember his face. Later, he would reward him. But, first, he would ask him why the hell he was relaxing in the seat among civilians. Good soldier, but lacking discipline.

He passed the cars. People stood out of his way. He met a few soldiers, and they saluted him. He answered each salute with pride. Yes, good soldiers, and he was an exceptional commander. No wonder. The military spirit flew in his veins. In his mind, Adlerstein thanked his father and his father's father, all the way back to the first known ancestor. Three hundred years of incredible commanders. The blood of warriors. That was why he'd gotten that fabulous idea of how to protect the prisoner. Whatever he did, it would end up with a positive result.

He reached the car dedicated to off-duty soldiers. They'd returned there immediately after defending the train. That had been his order. Many of them looked tired. They saluted, but their hands moved as if they were made of heavy stones. Adlerstein slowed his pace and observed. The recent military action had scared the shit out of them. It wasn't like drinking in Amsterdam's pubs and chasing hookers. This was real. A real battle with real fatalities. He passed them without saying a word and strode to the next car.

The rear guards lowered the submachine guns and saluted, raising their right hands.

"Everything all right here?" he said.

"Yes, Herr *Hauptsturmführer*."

"When did you change?"

"Twenty minutes ago, Herr *Hauptsturmführer*."

Adlerstein nodded and continued walking. One soldier opened the door to the gangway. It was always the same. One door, then the gangway, then the other door. Boring. *I should get an orderly. A reliable batman.*

The main guards in the prison car saluted. The prisoner lay on a seat covered with heavy military blankets. Just his head stuck out. He looked amused. A slight grin on his face.

"You think you won?" Adlerstein said, returning a sinister grin to the prisoner.

The British agent said nothing. He didn't even try to hide the fact that he was smiling.

"In a few hours, you will be delivered to the best hands in The Third Reich."

Nothing. Just a grin.

"Then you will beg for a fast death." His voice slowed down, emphasizing each syllable.

The prisoner provoked him, keeping his silence. Just not to burst out of anger. That would degrade his authority. The guards were watching.

"I will deliver you personally, and I will make sure you will suffer like never before," he said, lowering his voice. At the end of the sentence, he was hissing.

One of the soldiers chuckled. Adlerstein cast the most dangerous gaze he was capable of at him. The soldier's face reddened.

"I just wanted… His fate is sealed, Herr *Hauptsturmführer!*"

Adlerstein stepped closer and brought his face within an inch of him. The soldier's contours hazed, creating a dark silhouette on the bright background.

"Who asked you for your opinion?!"

The soldier swallowed hard and mumbled something.

"Who asked you for your opinion?" Adlerstein said, pointing out each word.

"Nobody, Herr *Hauptsturmführer.*" The soldier's voice was weak and trembled.

"What?!"

The soldier said nothing. His hazed face mixed with the background as it paled.

Adlerstein turned on his foot and strode back. After a few steps, he stopped and turned back to them.

"I want to see you when your duty is over! Do you understand?!"

The coupe Adlerstein reserved for himself in the rear half of the train felt crowded even though only three other officers occupied the seats. The air got heavy in a few minutes, lacking oxygen. Opening the window and letting the draft in would be risky because there was a pile of papers. Important documents. Adlerstein observed them without a word. Two *Untersturmführer,* and one *Ober-sturmführer.* They were like children, fidgeting and complaining about everything. They didn't deserve their ranks. He promised himself to find out where they had been during the attack. The prisoner was safe, but not because of them. Despite them.

"Listen carefully!" Adlerstein said in a sharp voice, interrupting their discussion.

The silence took over in an instant. Their faces. He would never forget their faces. Like a spoiled cat when someone took its chow away. He would teach them.

He continued, keeping his voice down. "I want you to take all your soldiers and do a deep security check on all passengers. Do you understand?"

"When?" one officer said.

"Now."

They gazed at each other as if he'd talked in a foreign language. No, it wasn't like they didn't understand. The was a lack of discipline. The pressure in Adlerstein's veins jumped up, and he felt the warmth of the blood red-dening his cheeks. His lungs whistled when he took a breath before yelling at them.

"I said I wanted you to take all your fucking soldiers and do a security check on all passengers now!" His last word took a high pitch. He had to take another breath. "Do you understand, or do I have to repeat it again?!"

The officers froze. Spoilt scumbags. Yelling released the tension in his throat, and his blood pressure declined. He couldn't breathe freely but suppressed the urge to open the door and let the fresh air in. Not now. Later. He was a soldier. He had to cope with discomfort.

"Questions?!"

Obersturmführer raised his hand, staring directly into his eyes.

"What it is, *Obersturmführer*?"

The man put down his hand and moved his sight aside.

"With all due respect, *Herr Hauptsturmführer*, I believe it would be a mistake to do so," *Obersturmführer* said in a low voice.

"Explain yourself."

"Let's imagine we do that. All soldiers will be spread over the train. That will weaken our position…"

"Weaken how?"

Obersturmführer gazed at him, his mouth opened.

"I asked you a question, *Obersturmführer*!"

"Yes. I… I assumed it was clear." He glanced at others, seeking help.

"No, it is not clear. Explain!"

"Well, the soldiers will be spread out, which means our power will be spread and weakened. I don't know how to explain it. We can expect another attack, and we should concentrate our forces. That's obvious." His voice regained confidence.

"Another attack? Yes, we can expect another attack. Maybe you didn't notice, but the machine guns I installed into the train's last car deflected the attack. Not by soldiers wasting their ammunition following your orders!"

Obersturmführer spread his arms. "Yes, because it was an air raid. What if the enemy attacks on the ground? They managed to stop the train once. They could do it again."

The other officers nodded, murmuring something under their breath. The rebellion. It had to be suppressed. Now, not later. Adlerstein pointed his finger at the officer.

"You're right on one point. They stopped the train, and they can do it again."

Obersturmführer shook his head. "They could. We don't know if they can."

"You don't know. I do. I know the enemy."

"Yes? Who is it? Can you name him?"

Adlerstein said nothing.

Obersturmführer continued. "I don't think we should waste the potential of our soldiers for doing a futile bust. The soldiers are tired; they need to rest before the next attack we can expect…"

The sound of his voice disappeared in Adlerstein's ears. Like he had a filter put inside. The only thing he perceived was the resistance that was getting more and more force. He found himself cracking his knuckles. It hurt, so he stopped. In his head, the picture of his hands pressing on *Obersturmführer's* throat unleashed a con-venient warmth flowing through his body. The image was so real that he felt the skin touch his fingers. A pulsating vein on his neck kicked him out of dreaming. The pressure was immense.

"Are you all right, *Hauptsturmführer*?"

"What?"

"Are you all right? You looked as if you were going to faint."

A bomb exploded inside Adlerstein. The pain was unbearable. He had to concentrate all the strength he had left.

"What the fuck are you talking about?" Adlerstein said in a low voice, slowly pronouncing each word.

All the officers stared at him.

"How do you dare to talk to me like that? Who are you?"

The silence inside the coupe became suffocating. Even the rattle of the car's wheels stopped. Adlerstein spoke up.

"I gave you an order, soldier! An order! And you? Instead of obeying, you rebel against me?" Thunders of his voice resonated the coupe's walls. The darkness spread in front of his eyes.

"Give me your gun!"

"What?"

"Your gun, *Obersturmführer!*"

"But why?"

"Because I told you so!"

"But why?"

Adlerstein said nothing, just held out his hand. *Obersturmführer* gazed around. The faces of other officers begged him to obey. It felt good. He, Adlerstein, knew how to compel obedience. They had to learn to discipline. He had to teach them.

Obersturmführer reached to his belt and drew his Luger, handing it to Adlerstein, who took it and checked the magazine. It was full, and the chamber was empty. This was how his officer had prepared himself for a battle, hiding himself in the shadows and praying for his gun not to fire. Coward. Traitor. He racked the slide.

"I'm demoting you, *Obersturmführer*," he said in a low voice.

"You have no right to do so."

"No right?! I will tell you what rights I do have. You're a traitor. You betrayed me, and therefore, you betrayed the Third Reich. Disobedience must be punished."

"I just expressed my opinion."

"You disobeyed."

Obersturmführer took a deep breath and gazed around again. Adlerstein grinned in his mind. *They won't help you!*

"My apologies, *Herr Hauptsturmführer*," he said in a low voice.

"It's too late to apologize."

Lightning flashed through *Obersturmführer's* eyes. The last moment of self-preservation. Adlerstein knew what was going to happen. He had seen this before. And he welcomed it.

Obersturmführer burst out. "Adlerstein, you have no right to demote me. Your behavior is inappropriate…"

Adlerstein grabbed him by his uniform and pulled him out of the seat, smashing his face against the door. The officer went limp, collapsing on the spot. In one fast move, Adlerstein opened the door to the corridor and threw *Obersturmführer* out. The man fell on the floor, lying on his belly. The others jumped from their seats, staring at Adlerstein when he stepped out. A few passengers stuck their heads out of the other coupes, but after assessing the situation, they pulled back and closed the doors.

"This is what will happen to anyone who disobeys me!"

He kneeled, flicked off the gun's safety with his thumb, and pressed it against *Obersturmführer's* head. Staring at other officers' faces, he pulled the trigger. Skull fragments mixed with brain matter splashed around the corridor's walls and the floor. *Obersturmführer's* body twitched. He was dead.

Adlerstein stood from the floor, still keeping his sights on the officers, whose skin went pale.

"Now, go and command your soldiers. I want to have results in one hour! Do you understand?"

They nodded and turned, striding away from him.

"Halt!" Adlerstein's voice drowned out the train's rumble.

They stiffened on the spot. After a few seconds, they turned to Adlerstein.

"Remember this moment for the rest of your lives," he said. "If you do, you will live longer than this traitor."

He saw them swallowed. "Now, go!"

"We are in the hands of a maniac." Adlerstein heard them whispering to each other while they ran down the corridor.

He grinned, satisfied with what he had just done. He had taught them discipline.

Chapter 12

The time was running around me. I wasted it. The prisoner was still in the prison car, and I spun in the same place, having no clue of what I should do or how I should proceed. I sat near the window in the car with other off-duty soldiers. After the next guards had changed us, I'd passed through all the passenger cars in this half of the train, up to the box car with machine guns, checking every coupe, every toilet and hoping I could find something. Something that would solve my problem or at least inspire me. Nothing. Sad thoughts took over my mind, fighting with me, and I was losing this battle. I'd done nothing so far. At least biting my nails would be something, but I hadn't even done that. I wanted to check on the prisoner, but I hadn't found an opportunity to get there. I couldn't just walk in. I needed a good reason; otherwise, they would send me back, and I didn't want to point a gun at them before I knew how ready they were to fire back.

The cars' rattling cut through my brain, kicking me out of my thoughts. It was suddenly getting on my nerves. I hated it.

The other soldiers relaxed, lying, or sitting wherever possible and discussing the air raid. The excitement rush overtaking the tiredness. Their first real action in this war. Feeling miserable, I went to the toilet.

When I returned, *Unterscharführer,* who led our squad, was giving orders. The soldiers stood in a circle around him.

I pulled Stefan by his shoulder. "What's going on here?"

"New orders," he whispered.

"What orders?" I whispered back.

He turned his head to me and put his finger on his lips. "Shhh."

"Don't shush me," I said, speaking up.

Unterscharführer and the rest of the soldiers frowned, casting devil's eyes at me.

"Müller, do you want to say it instead of me?!" the *Unterscharführer* said.

"No."

"Then keep your dirty mouth shut!" All soldiers changed their sights back to *Unterscharführer,* and he continued. I didn't listen.

"Who gave new orders?" I said, whispering into Stefan's ear.

"Adlerstein."

"Have you ever met him? What does he look like?"

"No, I haven't. I guess he looks like an SS officer," Stefan said, keeping his eyes on *Unterscharführer*.

"Oh, yes, that helped my imagination a lot," I said and turned away.

"Müller, again?!" *Unterscharführer* said.

"I'm sorry," I said.

"Sorry? You are not at school, soldier! You're in the army. No one gives a shit about your sorries."

"All right."

Unterscharführer grinned like a father who'd caught his son smoking a cigarette but remembered that he was the same at his son's age.

"And because you're so smart, I want you, Fischer, and here, *Oberschütze*, to go to the first car to check passengers."

"Thank you, Müller. Now I have to go through all the cars. Thank you!" *Oberschütze* said.

"Your legs won't drop off your body. Don't be scared," Stefan said.

Oberschütze pulled his head deeper between his shoulders and kept silent. I didn't like that man. He was such a numbskull who had always made things worse instead of fixing them.

Unterscharführer returned to others. "Don't forget. We are looking for a British spy, but it can be a Dutch or a German with proper documents…"

"*Unterscharführer*?"

"Yes, Müller?"

"Why we need to go there like three soldiers?"

"What you mean? It always must be three soldiers. What did they teach you in the training camp?"

"Saluting," I said, casting provoking sights at him.

He didn't respond to my challenge. "Two soldiers aim their rifles at the person while the third soldier checks the papers. And don't ask such stupid questions again, or I will kick your ass until it becomes a marmalade! You've got your training, soldier!"

All the soldiers chuckled, and we left, each patrol to its position. Fortune decided to play nice with me and gave me an opportunity to examine the prison car.

Only a few seats had been removed. The partitions separating the vestibule in the middle from the seat sections were also disassembled. The car looked like the guard car, but it had more seats.

We strolled through. Everyone was curious about the spy. There was nothing to see, though. A big pile of military blankets. When I turned my head, I spotted the face of a man in his fifties with a thick gray mustache. The face looked familiar, but I couldn't assign it to anyone I knew. The signalization button dangled on the twisted wires that hung over the handle. I reached with my hand to examine it, but one guard pushed me so strongly I almost fell to the floor. For a second, I thought I'd unveiled my true intentions. Everything was getting on my nerves. I had to calm down. There were more important things to answer than the signalization. Like, why so many blankets? Did they expect it would prevent the prisoner from receiving a bullet? That would be stupid. Or was he injured and wrapped in the blankets to keep him warm? Was he in any condition to jump off the train?

The following car with the vanguards looked like a mirror of ours. The guards closed the gangway door behind us, and *Oberschütze* had a small talk with one of them. They said nothing important, just exchanged a few words about the weather, and promised to have a beer in a Berlin pub. Evidently, they knew each other. I didn't give a shit about them. Now, I knew that freeing the prisoner would ask for a lot of blood. There was no place for tricks. Just kill everyone and kill them quickly, not giving them an opportunity to shoot or call for help by pressing that stupid signalization button before I would get them.

The passengers in the other cars we passed through welcomed us with fear. I spotted a face I thought I knew and accidentally hit the metallic frame of one seat with my submachine gun. The sharp click made people stiffen. They lost all the blood from under their skin. Many of them cowered, expecting terror. I tried to cast an apologetic look at them, but it didn't work. The gray uniform was connected with fear, and it couldn't be removed by grinning at them.

On the other hand, the last car we got in, the mail car, was full of joy. An older German mailman welcomed us with a big smile on his face. He offered a cup of tea from the teapot, which I accepted, letting him pour the hot beverage into the steel military cup all soldiers were equipped with. *Oberschütze* gazed at me as if I had eaten his dinner, but said nothing. He was a coward, and I was willing to use it without having bad feelings, without remorse.

"So, how's Hitler doing? Is he still hiding his second ball?" the mailman said.

I burst into laughter, spluttering tea around me, while Stefan just chuckled and shrank under the serious gaze of *Oberschütze*.

"You shouldn't say such things," *Oberschütze* said.

"Why? Hitler has just one ball. That's a fact. I can tell the facts anytime," the mailman said and sipped his tea.

They locked eyes. My heart beat. It was exciting to observe them. The mailman, perhaps a seventy-year-old energetic bloke on the one side, and on the other side, a stupid coward whose power lay only in his gun. I pulled my MP40, ready to shoot at *Oberschütze*. I didn't need to, though.

"I can arrest you for that, you know?"

"You can arrest my ass, son. Don't be stupid and sip your tea. Enjoy a moment when you don't need to pretend loyalty." The old man grinned and winked. "Don't worry. I won't tell anyone."

"You just insulted our *Führer*."

"He insulted me when he started acting like an idiot. He and his government." The mailman turned to me. "I admit, I voted for him in the first elections when he lost. His speeches were full of enthusiasm and compassion. To the country. To the people whose lives became miserable because of the first war. He wanted to build roads and houses and reward veterans. Fix the economy. Fix our fucked existences."

He tilted his head, and his voice got sad.

"Yes. But then he started to show his true face. And when he fooled the masses and won the elections, I left the country. Ashamed."

I liked this old man.

Oberschütze couldn't cope with the truth. He put his cup aside and stood, racking the slide on his gun. The gun pointed at the mailman. The old man didn't hesitate and jumped to his feet. He grabbed the gun's barrel and pressed it against his chest.

"If you want to shoot me, son, do it now or sit back and finish your tea," the old man said in a low but firm voice. Energy radiated from him.

"I'm not afraid of you, son. I fought for our country in the first war and saw things that would make you piss your bed every night if you had seen them. That funny toy of yours you are pointing at me won't make me bend. You are now in my kingdom."

They stood there for a while. *Oberschütze* avoided a direct gaze at the veteran. He broke and lowered the submachine gun, and the mailman released the barrel from his grip.

"I have more important problems to deal with than you, old man. I will let you go for now. I respect you're a veteran."

The mailman laughed. "You have respect for nothing but your scared ass, you piece of shit. Now, sit and finish your tea. I won't hurt you, don't worry, although I killed more men than you can imagine."

Oberschütze jerked as if he wanted to say something, but the mailman's voice lashed in the air like a whip. "Sit!"

Oberschütze resembled a good-trained dog for a moment and parked his ass on the hard wooden chair.

The silence entered the mail car. I observed Stefan. His eyes jumped from side to side, gazing at the mailman and then at *Oberschütze*. His breath went fast and then slowed down. He held his cup to his lips but didn't sip. Stefan fought with himself, and I saw it.

We finished our cups and stood. Turning around, I spotted big glass bottles in the corner. They were full of liquid.

"What are those?" I said.

The mailman turned his head and shrugged. "I have no idea. Someone is sending something to Berlin." He grinned. "Maybe, it's a schnapps. Or a plum brandy."

I stepped closer. The labels were written in small letters, so I had to bend to read them. Ammonium sulfide! The stinky bomb. Why would someone send it by mail? Then I remembered what I'd heard about it, and it made sense. Ammonium sulfide was used as a fertilizer. The label carried the name of a producer from Am-sterdam.

I turned to the mailman. "It's ammonium sulfide. Be careful. I would move those bottles aside and wrap them with something soft if I were you."

"Why?"

"If just one bottle cracks, you won't be happy, believe me. It's a stink bomb. It stinks more than a thousand shits."

He laughed. "Really?"

I nodded.

"Well, thanks for the advice. I'll move them. It's my kingdom, and I don't want to it stinking like sewage."

We shook hands and left. I couldn't stop thinking about Stefan.

Chapter 13

We crossed the gangway and stepped into the empty car's vestibule. I was last and closed the door. *Oberschütze* spun toward me and Stefan, shooting daggers from his eyes.

"I would expect you to back me up!"

"Stop talking and move on," I said.

He raised his finger. "I will report what happened to *Scharführer.*"

I said nothing, waiting for him to finish.

"This is unacceptable. We are to be respected by civilians. Even by old veterans."

"You will report nothing."

He frowned and took one step closer to me, trying to look dangerous. This bully coward expected me to shit my trousers. He had bent before the old mailman, and that had made him sick. Now, he wanted to pour his anger on us. A falling shit.

I grabbed the collar of his uniform and smashed him to the wall, pressing on his chest with my forearm.

"You will report nothing, do you understand?"

His face reflected mixed emotions. I spotted the anger of losing authority and the fear of getting his lips split. I lifted my hand and pressed the barrel of my MP40 under his chin.

"Otherwise, I'll shoot your brain out of your stupid head," I said.

He swallowed.

"Do you understand?"

He nodded.

"Say it."

"I understand," he said in a low voice. Not giving up, he searched for help from Stefan, but Stefan didn't even notice what was happening. His head was tilted down as if his soul flew far away in the deep places in his con-sciousness.

"All right. Now we will pretend how busy we are checking all the passengers. But we will leave them be. Do you understand?"

"I understand."

"Good," I said and released his uniform.

His cowardice won and took over his mind. *Oberschütze* fixed his shirt, tucking it into his trousers. It had pulled out when I grabbed him.

"Ready?" I said.

He nodded.

"Let's go!" I opened the door.

Stefan woke up. He looked confused. I let him be. This was his battle, not mine.

The check was boring. People showed us their papers. No one resisted. From time to time, I looked at the document over the *Oberschütze*'s shoulder. Everything was in order. Despite the war, people were still trying to live their lives. They traveled when they needed to. They got their documents as requested. I just couldn't under-stand why it was so important to have them. A child could fake a piece of paper. The only purpose was to spread fear among citizens. To create a feeling of being controlled. We passed the car, entered the next, and played the same game.

Oberschütze was getting tired. His gestures weakened. The skin on his face got loose.

"We don't need to check everyone," I said, whispering into his ear.

He raised his brows at me. "We must. If an SS secret agent or someone from the Gestapo sees us neglecting the checks, we will have a big problem," he said.

"Fuck them all. I'm getting bored by this."

"Me too, but I don't want to take the risk."

"Let's have a break."

I sat on a free seat. *Oberschütze*, seeing me, sat on the opposite seat. Stefan stood there, his palms grasping the MP40. He didn't notice we were sitting.

"Stefan, are you with us?"

He came out of the trance. "What?"

"I just asked if you are here," I said, grinning.

"Yes, yes. Don't worry," He lowered the submachine gun, putting it behind his back, and sat across the aisle right before a young couple.

"Are you traveling to Berlin?" he said grinning at them.

The man said nothing, just handed the documents to him.

Stefan shook his head and waved his hand in a refusing gesture. "I don't want to see your papers."

Oberschütze straightened his back, but my stern gaze stopped him.

Stefan insisted, waving his hand. "No, put the papers back in your pocket."

He tilted his head down, staring at the floor. A young boy playing with a wooden horse jumped off his seat and approached him, handing him his toy. Stefan took it, grooming the wooden horse's hair. The boy laughed, hopping on one leg. This was Stefan's world. I saw it. Being a teacher who knew how to talk to children, not a soldier with a gun.

Still stretching his hand with papers, the young man gazed at me, and I nodded. "Do as he said. We don't need to see your papers."

The man's face relaxed. His fiancée, or perhaps his wife, pushed closer to him, finding shelter under his arm.

"Don't worry. No one will harm you," I said with a strong feeling that whatever I would say was futile. The sadness of my powerlessness to change people's minds tried to take over my mind, but I resisted. I had to relax and focus on my task.

I checked *Oberschütze*. He looked as if he was waiting for my command to continue, but at the same time, he desired to excuse his cowardice.

"We don't need to rush," he said.

I nodded and cast a grin at the young couple. For a moment, I forgot there was a war.

The train slowed down, reaching the next station when the vestibule door opened, and a man in a black hat entered.

"They got some spy or…" He froze when he spotted us.

I stood from my seat. "Go on. What's happening?"

He hesitated but continued, "A patrol found someone without papers." He pointed his finger. "In that car."

I gazed at *Oberschütze*. "We need to go and check what happened."

He shook his head, hugging his gun. "No. We need to stay here."

I waved my hand and strode toward the back of the car. Stefan followed.

"Halt!" said *Oberschütze*. "Don't go there. It means trouble."

I turned to him. "Trouble for an innocent man."

"No, if they found a spy… I don't want to mess with them."

"You don't need to. Just sit here and shit your pants," I said, turning away from him.

Some people chuckled.

"You put us in danger. They got a spy."

I spun on the spot. "They have an innocent man, can't you see it?"

"There's a spy!"

"There's no spy!"

I grabbed the door handle. Out of the corner of my eye, I saw him jumping to his feet and running behind me and Stefan.

We crossed the gangway when the train stopped at the station. I opened the gangway door and flinched back. The vestibule was full of people waiting to get out. Someone opened the door to the outside, and the mass poured out of the train, leaving us alone. Through the glass on the door leading to the car's aisle, I spotted a man kneeling on the floor. The door rumbled when I kicked it open.

All faces glanced at me. A few passengers occupying the seats sat breathless. One soldier was aiming his submachine gun at the kneeling man, while the second one aimed at the passengers. *Oberscharführer* was talking to the man, bending over him. I strode there.

"What is happening?" I said.

"We arrested a spy," *Oberscharführer* said, casting a gaze full of pride.

I turned at the man kneeling on the floor. "Are you a British spy?" I said in English, laughing in my mind. I couldn't find anything better to ask.

"*Je ne comprends pas ce que vous me demandez. Je suis le français niçois et je voyage à Berlin pour rencontrer mon frère.*" the man said in a low, trembling voice. He pressed his palms together as if he was praying. I spotted tears in his eyes. His face was a map of fear. This man was innocent. No one could pretend such a face.

"Does it sound to you like the English language?" I said, gazing at the officer.

"That proves nothing. He can understand and play the game with us. What did you ask him?"

I ignored his question. "He's a Frenchman from Nice who is traveling to Berlin to meet his brother. Look at him!"

The officer cast a gaze full of disgust at me. "I don't care what he says. Soldiers! Take him to the prison car."

Two soldiers stopped pointing their MP40s but didn't grab the Frenchman yet, waiting to see what would happen next.

Oberscharführer turned. "You speak English and French." He pointed his finger at me. "I don't like it, and I don't like you!"

Stefan opened his mouth. "Yes, you don't like educated people. I speak English and French, too. And Latin. And ancient Greek. Do you like me?" Stefan didn't wait for the answer and turned toward the man on the floor. "*Parles-vous anglais*? Do you speak English?"

The man shook his head.

"*Avez-vous des documents?* Do you have documents?"

"*Je les avais mais je les ai perdus.* I had them but lost them."

"*Ce qui s'est passé?* What happened?"

"*Je ne sais pas, j'ai peur. Je voyage à Berlin pour rencontrer mon frère.* I don't know, I'm scared. I'm travelling to Berlin to meet my brother."

"Can't you see this man is not a British spy? He's innocent," I said.

All passengers hummed when they heard the word 'spy.' The officer stepped closer to me. I smelled his stin-ky breath.

"Do I look like I give a shit, *Schütze?*"

My hand jerked back, but Stefan grabbed my shoulder and stopped the explosion. I thanked him in my mind. My temper could reveal my intentions.

"This man is innocent. Just a passenger going to Berlin." Stefan said to the officer.

"I should kick your ass, *Schütze.* But I'm in a good mood. He has no papers. That's a problem." He chuckled. "His problem."

The vestibule door slammed. *Untersturmführer* entered, striding toward us.

"What's going on here?!"

Everyone saluted. I barely waved my hand. Raising my hand as expected, I would vomit. No one noticed.

The *Oberscharführer* reported. The face of *Untersturmführer* remained hardened. He listened to each word, gazing at the Frenchman from time to time.

"Take him!" he said.

The soldiers grabbed the Frenchman, pulling him onto the platform. The passengers and us glued ourselves to the windows.

The Frenchman was like a lamb in the hands of SS soldiers. Timid and yielding. He obeyed all their commands and let himself be led. They stopped on the platform and forced him to kneel. Although, his knees buckled under the lightest pressure of their hands. The soldiers' grip softened.

Suddenly, the Frenchman sprang to his feet and began to run. *Untersturmführer* pulled his Luger out and aimed. The shot cracked through the air like a whip, fading away. In an instant, all the windows opened, and everyone stuck their heads out, stretching their necks to see whether the bloke had fallen dead. Nothing like that happened, though. The Frenchman lay on the ground, shot in the leg. Two soldiers ran there and stood him up.

Untersturmführer barked the order, and they dragged the poor bloke to the back of the train. His wounded leg painted a thin red curved line.

Chapter 14

All passengers and we were still at windows, watching the Frenchman being dragged toward the prison car. I didn't like what had happened. I knew that many people had disappeared or been murdered by this stupid, totalitarian regime. But seeing it with my own eyes was a different experience. Could I have helped him? Could I have done more to prevent this from happening?

Oberschütze stepped closer to me and put his hand on my shoulder.

"There's nothing you could do. Let it be. That's his fate," he said in a voice I hadn't heard for ages.

I turned my head and gazed at him. He reminded me of a father calming his son who'd fallen off a bicycle for the first time. I wanted to punch him, to hit him hard, stamp on him. Break all his bones. It would only help my anger, though. It wouldn't save the Frenchman or the British spy. On the contrary, it might ruin the task I was here for. So, instead of punching him in the face, I turned away. He got it and took his hand off.

The train was still waiting at the station.

"What are we waiting for?" I said, turning toward Stefan.

"Don't know. Probably, they need to refill the water and wood," he said, watching through the window.

"Nonsense. They did it in the previous station."

Oberschütze joined our conversation. "I think our commanders are interrogating the Frenchman. That's why we wait."

I sighed. "You better shut your fucking mouth, or I will do it on your behalf."

"You're mad at me? What should I have done, huh? There was no way to save him."

I ignored him. This pants-shitter wasn't worth my attention. But he couldn't stop and nudged my shoulder with his palm.

"Huh? What would you do?"

I still ignored him.

"I'm doing what I can. I don't want to mess with anybody. Don't you understand that? To me, I'm more important than some Frenchman."

He nudged me again. I turned. He gazed down at me. I kneed him in the balls with my right knee. He fell to the floor. It all took one second. I wasn't proud of what I had done but felt relief. The tension in my mind eased.

The passenger observed us but said nothing. No one stood up for him. The reality touched my senses and shook my consciousness. They would have reacted the same way if I had been in his position. *Oberschütze* sat on the seat and pressed his palms against his crotch. He pushed his knees together and swayed, keeping his head down.

The vestibule door opened, and an SS soldier came in, striding right toward us.

"Have you heard?" he said.

"No. Do you have some news?" Stefan said.

The bloke nodded, eager to share his knowledge. "*Hauptsturmführer* Adlerstein sent men to the local *Wehrmacht* base for a truck."

"A truck? Why does he need a truck?"

"I don't know. I think our journey on the train has ended. Everyone hopes we will get back to Amsterdam." He grinned, rubbing his hands together.

"How ended? The *Wehrmacht* will take the prisoner?" I said.

"No. I don't think so."

"Then?"

"One officer said Adlerstein would escort the prisoner on the truck."

"Alone?"

He shook his head and tapped his forehead with his fingers. "Of course, not alone. How could you ask such a stupid question?"

"You said our journey has ended."

"It has."

I shrugged and turned away. This bloke would never get that if his information were accurate, some soldiers would continue with Adlerstein on the truck.

But, if it were true, I would have to change my direction. My stomach tensed. How would I get on the truck? I couldn't give up. I had to do something. If they asked for volunteers, I would be the first in a row. I had to be. Or I could spoil the truck. What a good idea. Then Adlerstein would have to continue on the train. Another possibility was to replace the driver. Would I be able to free the spy if I were a driver? Probably yes. I could expect Adlerstein to be in the truck cab with me. Easy target, though. And then pull the truck off the road and shoot the escort. Hard to do without hitting the spy. And how to let Simon know about the change? I hoped he would follow the train. Considering everything, the train still looked like the best option. This planning without having proper information led to nowhere. I had to see the truck. Then, I would make a decision and change the plan if necessary.

Without a word, I turned and sneaked out of the car. I expected the truck to arrive at the street in front of the station. I had to keep one eye on the train, though. Not to miss it if it suddenly started to move. *Fucking complications!*

The truck arrived. The driver made a U-turn before the building and reversed into the grass at the side of the station. The station building covered it, hiding it from any observing eyes on the train. That was good. A *Wehrmacht Leutnant*, *Obergefreiter*, and about twenty soldiers jumped off the truck's bed and marched toward the train. Most of the soldiers bent under the weight of heavy metal boxes. The driver stayed in the truck. That was bad.

I decided to harm the truck as much as possible. It was old, so I didn't expect it to be hard work. The more time they would need to fix the damage, the better. It would convince Adlerstein to change his plans and continue on the train. Puncturing each tire and cutting all the hoses and pipes on the engine. A hole in the tank. A million possibilities.

The sun was frying the air, and I sweated under the uniform. The sooner I finished, the better. I secured my MP40 on my back, drew the knife from my boot, and then, I crept to the rear axle, checking on any movements and sounds. No one noticed. The driver was still in the cab, whistling some song. He kept the engine running. I kneeled at the truck's duals and pulled back my hand to stab the outer tire, but I froze. It could explode and lure the driver, attracting his attention. Pressing the blade against the corner of the tire, I cut through it. The pressure tore the edges, and the air escaped.

Holding my breath, I listened to the driver. His whistling continued uninterrupted. The engine purred happily. Good. Five more, and I was done. I had no idea how to puncture the front tires. I didn't think about it, though. Encouraged by the small success, I began to cut the second tire on this side of the truck. My sharp knife did a good job, and after a few seconds, the air blew out, but the truck leaned to the side. Almost at the same time, the front door slammed, and I spotted a pair of legs strolling toward the truck's back. A rough voice coursed in German. I rolled underneath the truck.

"*Scheize!*" he said when he stepped next to the damaged wheels.

I crawled toward the front axle, praying the punctured tires would entertain him long enough for me to get from under the truck and run along it to its back on the other side. I planned to attack him from behind.

"*Was machst du hier?!* What are you doing here?!" His voice rumbled in the narrow space.

I rolled to the side and jumped on my feet. He straighttened and turned toward me. Seeing me grasping the knife, he lowered his body, ready to defend himself. For one second, we just stood there, our eyes locked. He wore the light *Wehrmacht* uniform and wasn't much taller than me. Rolled sleeves revealed he had strong muscular arms. A gift from spinning the truck's steering wheel.

I leaped forward and sprung my hand, aiming the knife at his neck. He blocked my lunge with ease, as if he did it every day. In the next quarter of a second, he grabbed my wrist and jerked me forward, tilting his head down for a headbutt. My nose hurt. The world around me faded in an instant, and for a second, I lost the perception of my surroundings. A dark silhouette swung its hand, and a sharp pain burst from my forearm bones, making me release the knife. This man knew how to fight. Three seconds, perhaps less, and I was without a knife but had darkness in front of my eyes. Another swing of the arm and his fist landed on my temple. My knees buckled, and I fell to the ground, hitting it hard with the back of my head. The MP40, still on my back, stung between my shoulder blades.

Like some miracle, instead of sending me uncon-sciousness, it poured a new energy into my body. My sight sharpened, the pain in my nose and forearm faded. The driver stood between my legs, pulling his gun from the holster on his belt. Walther P38. I swept my left leg around, hooking him under the knees and knocking him down.

In one fluid motion, I sprang and landed on him. I grabbed his wrist with both hands before he could cock the gun. In the following seconds, we fought for the gun, pulling each other's hands up and down. His arm was stronger than I thought. With his free palm, he pushed my head backward, pressing against my face, and jerked up his pistol-holding hand. That sudden move stretched my arms and weakened my grip. The sharp metallic sound of the gun cocking rang out like a boxing ring's gong at the end of the round. Turning my head, I freed my face from his palm and smashed my fist into his elbow, using my neck as a lever. It wasn't strong enough to break the elbow joint, but sufficient to cause pain. He screamed and instinctively grabbed his injured elbow.

I yanked his wrist holding the gun down and twisted it. The shot thundered in the space, and a crimson stain developed on his chest. His resistance faded, and I fell over his dead body. *Shit!* Not the result I wanted. Everyone must have heard that. What now?

I had a little time to finish this bloody task. The gun was still in his hand. I opened his fingers and took it. The magazine was full, minus one bullet. Crouching under the truck, I shot into all wheels. I didn't mind the noise anymore. Shooting was faster than cutting through the rubber with a knife. The truck would stay here for a long time.

My knife glittered in the grass next to the truck. I grabbed it and opened the truck's hood. A thin brass tubes led to the side of the engine. The fuel pipelines for the injectors. I cut them apart. The engine's roar stopped. The stench of diesel filled the air. This all took five seconds.

I glanced at the dead driver. A crazy thought flashed through my mind. This could discourage Adlerstein or whoever would make a decision. I lifted the heavy body and put it on the engine. His gun followed. I didn't need it. The hood closed without resisting. Now, they could look for the driver till the morning.

I ran toward the entrance to the station. Behind the corner, I halted and peeked out. A group of *Wehrmacht* soldiers led by *Obergefreiter* returned to the truck. All of them held submachine guns in a position ready to fire. I held my breath. My heart pounding from fatigue. *Obergefreiter* checked the empty truck cab. Something attracted his attention. He jumped down and bent over the spot on the ground. I knew what it was. Blood. He shouted commands, and the soldiers scattered in all directions. One bloke ran back to the train.

I strode around the station building. Hidden behind the corner, I fixed my uniform, tucking the shirt into the trousers. The MP40 returned to my waist. My panting ceased, and my heart calmed. A blood stain decorated my left arm. I didn't care. The task was secured.

Chapter 15

Hauptsturmführer Adlerstein smashed his fist on the small table installed in his coupe beneath the window. The *Wehrmacht* officer, *Leutnant*, who had told him the sad news blinked and stepped backward. His pale face reflecting a sudden desire to disappear. Adlerstein ignored him and turned away, gazing through the window. Those fuckers spoiled whatever they touched! What now? He had thought that there had been only one British agent on the train, but now, he was sure there were many. One person couldn't have done it all. The Frenchman was innocent; that was as clear as the sky on a sunny day. He had cried before Adlerstein had used any of the proven methods to make someone talk. He shit his trousers. No agent would've done that.

"Who said the truck is not functional?" Adlerstein said.

"Me."

Adlerstein turned at him.

"I inspected the truck. All the tires are shot. The truck can't move."

"And the *Wehrmacht* has no other trucks?"

"Not a one, *Herr Hauptsturmführer.*"

"Not even a spare tire."

"No, *Herr Hauptsturmführer.*"

The sudden anger shook his mind. "How come that the army of The Third Reich has only one truck?" His voice rose.

The officer took one more step back. "We are a small base, just settling down in this area. Twenty-five soldiers and *Oberst,* plus me."

Adlerstein's eyes cast lightning. "You are not useful to me, *Leutnant.* Usually, I get rid of useless things."

That was an insult. He wanted to insult this moron from the *Wehrmacht.* He wished the officer would've stood up and defended his dignity. He wanted to kill him on this very spot.

The officer's pose changed. His shoulders bent back, and his chest rose. "Your threats mean nothing to me, *Herr Hauptsturmführer.* I am a *Wehrmacht* officer! The *Wehrmacht* won this country, not the SS!" he said in a sharp voice and moved his hand toward the holster on his belt, gripping the pistol's handle.

That was the gesture of a coward. Adlerstein despised cowards. Taking advantage in a duel. Primitive. Shooting before the countdown. How dishonorable.

The officer droned on about the *Wehrmacht's* superiority over the others, but Adlerstein didn't listen.

That chicken wasn't important anymore. He waved him away and turned back at the window. After a while, the door slammed. Outside, civilians strolled over the platform, nervous to get back to their seats. He knew he had to continue on the train. Fixing the truck would take a long time. He better focused on securing the train. Any of those people could've been an agent. But who? He felt a strong urge to execute them all. Men, women, and children. Everyone should stand against the wall facing the barrels of the execution squad.

Adlerstein sat, stretching his legs under the opposite seat, and lit a cigarette. The smoke scattered in the coupe, hazing the dark red curtains on the door. The more smoke he blew out, the darker the curtain became. A shy idea appeared in the corner of his mind. He let it strengthen. The well-known warmth of victory poured over his body. The dopamine rush. He felt it from his feet up to his head. Yes, that would do.

"Wagner!"

Nothing happened. Where the hell is that bloody man? Adlerstein opened the door and peeked at the corridor. Two soldiers were arguing just a few meters from his coupe.

"Wagner! What the fuck are you doing? Are you deaf?"

Both soldiers jumped and saluted.

"Come over, you stupid moron!" he said and returned to the coupe.

"*Jawohl!*" The soldier saluted at the door.

"Go and tell all commanders to drive all passengers to the front half of the train. Do you understand?"

"*Jawohl, Herr Hauptsturmführer!* All passengers to the front of the train!"

"And tell the guards commander only officers can enter the prison car. One officer will always be present during the guard change."

The soldier nodded.

"And I need guards in the mail car. No civilians can enter it."

"*Jawohl, Herr Hauptsturmführer!* Guards in the mail car."

"Go!"

The soldier clacked his heels, raised his right hand, and ran away.

Good idea. It would eliminate the enemy's activities. They wouldn't be able to do anything. He should have gone and given orders by himself, but he had no time. Just moving all the passengers would take ages. Meanwhile, he could prepare for the strongest trump hiding up his sleeve. He bared his teeth in a menacing grin. Yes, it was true. He, Adlerstein, was unstoppable.

Chapter 16

Running along the station building farther back, I approached the train from behind. No one could tell that I had been at the truck fighting with the driver a few minutes ago. People stood on the overcrowded platform, talking and gesturing. It looked like everyone got off the train. No wonder the shooting lured them out. They would have a subject for discussion for several weeks. I paid no attention to it. Then, things got better. What I'd done should be enough. Enough to keep the prisoner on the train. Enough to convince Adlerstein to continue to Berlin on the railroad.

Strolling forward, I couldn't move without zigzagging between the passengers standing there. More and more people got on the platform. Through the window, I spotted a bunch of soldiers inside the car giving orders and pointing with their hands toward the outside. Something was happening. This wasn't just a curiosity.

I stopped by a soldier who was picking up papers from the ground. Evidently, a passenger had bumped into him. "What's happening?"

He lifted his head, squinting at the sun. "We got orders to move all passengers to the front half of the train. Where have you been? Sleeping?"

I ignored his question. "All passengers? Why?"

He stood up, leveling the papers he'd already picked up. "I don't know. Ask Adlerstein. His orders, not mine. I've got only problems with his stupid orders."

"Thanks!" I strolled forward, leaving him there.

"Wait! Where have you been?"

Still moving, I turned to him. "I've got a secret mission. Can't talk about it."

He spat on the rails and crouched again.

Adlerstein fought with me, even though we hadn't yet met each other. Would his new move harm my plan? Probably wouldn't. No, it wouldn't. My plan was to find a way to free the prisoner. He didn't know about me. He just did what he found to be useful for him. I looked around. The passengers and the soldiers. How many sol-diers? All of them? This was an opportunity. The guards could have had no one to signal to. I could attack, shoot them, and jump out on the other side. The soldiers were occupied with moving passengers. The chance of es-caping unnoticed was high. The train made no noise, though. Everyone would hear shooting. I had to check on the situation. I had to get to the prison car using whatever excuse I could come up with.

I tried the door of the prison car, but both doors were locked. Going straight through the gangway sounded like a good idea. The stairs were dismounted, but I could reach the railings and pull myself up, supporting my feet on the piece of metal under the gangway. Crouching, I got closer to the door. When I reached out and grabbed the door handle, the opposite door opened, and a soldier from the rearguard pointed his MP40 at me. I knew his face. The bloke was from 'my squad.'

"What are you doing here?"

"I should ask you the same question," I said.

"Go away, or I will shoot."

"Come on, you won't shoot at me, right?"

"I won't if you make no problems."

I spread my hands. "Is it normal for you to threaten everyone from your squad?"

"We got new orders. No one can pass through. Only officers."

At lightning speed, I grabbed my submachine gun and racked the slide.

"Yeah, what now?"

His face got pale, and his mouth fell open.

"You didn't expect this twist of the situation, did you?" I said.

He said nothing but slowly raised his hands.

"Oh, don't be silly and put your hands down. I don't want to shoot you."

I couldn't shoot him. Noise.

He released his hands. "Why the hell did you do that?"

"I wanted to show you how hard it is to point a gun at me, all right?"

He nodded.

"Why are you so nervous?" I said.

"We haven't been changed yet."

"How come?"

"I should have been off duty one hour ago."

"One hour ago?" I tried to cast a buddy face. "Now, turn, go back, wait for the next shift, and let me be. I have my orders, too."

The door behind me burst open. I twisted. Another soldier, this time from the guards in the prison car, stood there.

"Go away, you idiot! We have orders to shoot. Go away!"

I couldn't defend myself between two MP40s aiming at me. Not without being shot. Or killed. I had way better ideas on how to die. Being shot by two Nazis wasn't on my list. In my mind, I grinned when I imagined them shooting each other. Not all bullets would end up in my body.

The bloke continued. "I saw you sniffing around. You tried to open the side door. I don't know what you're up to, but I'm tellin' you. Go away!"

I gave up and, without a word of explanation, I jumped down from the gangway onto the platform. I had to find some other way to get there. Now, the guards are more vigilant. Waiting for the guards to change sounded like a great idea. The next shift would be easier to fool.

The train was on the move again. I strolled through the empty cars in the rear half. Two of them had coupes along the corridor, the rest were ordinary cars like the ones in the front half, without the middle vestibule. They had vestibules and toilets at each end, though. Now, I understood how Adlerstein arranged the train. All added cars had a middle vestibule. Then, the unmounted seats and disassembled partitions created open space for a battle. A potential enemy was exposed to the fire after entering the car. Quite clever. I had to admit that.

I met a few groups of soldiers. We nodded heads in greeting. When I entered the corridor of the next car, I spotted a man jumping into the coupe. The third coupe. He had no uniform. I darted after him. The door was open, and he welcomed me by holding his hands before him. His face full of fear. He took two steps back when I stood at the door holding the submachine gun pointed at him.

"Don't shoot!" he said in German. But it was a strange German accent I'd never heard before.

"Don't shoot," he said again, this time more whispering than speaking.

"What are you doing here?"

"I'm traveling to Berlin."

"I know that, you're not going to the moon. What are you doing in this car? Every passenger was moved to the front."

He spread his arms. "I was sleeping."

"You were what?!" This couldn't have been real.

"I was sleeping. I fell asleep soon after the train left Amsterdam and woke up a few minutes ago."

"Did you hide somewhere?"

"No. I was here." He pointed his finger at the seat by the window.

"And no one saw you? Really?"

He shrugged. "I don't know. When I woke up, the car was empty."

"Not even the plane woke you up?"

He shook his head. "A plane? I heard some noise, but I was exhausted."

He looked comical. And risked his life, though. If the soldiers got him, he would be in big trouble. More likely dead.

"You must go to the front of the train," I said. My MP40 was still pointing at him. I lowered it and strapped it across my back. This bloke wouldn't shoot at me.

"Why?"

I closed the curtains on the coupe's door and sat on the seat, gesturing for him to sit down. He did so and dragged his feet under. He was taller than me. His clothes were worn. The brown wool jacket was too tight for him and stank of sweat and dirt. It hadn't seen a washboard in ages. The man left it unbuttoned. And his funny dark blue fedora hat. The brown trousers hung on him, though, secured with an old belt.

"Why?" he asked again.

"All passengers were moved."

"You've already told me that, and I still don't know why I should go to the front of the train."

"If they catch you here, you will be executed."

He leaned a bit forward. "They?"

"The SS troops."

"Are you not an SS soldier?" he said and put down the hat he wore. The man had a military haircut.

I pulled the gun strap and grabbed the MP40, pointing it at him again. "Who are you? Tell the truth."

Gazing into the barrel, he changed his behavior. He bent back, leaning on the seatback, and lifted his hands again.

"Don't shoot, please."

"I will repeat my question only once. Who are you?"

It took him a while to answer. I watched his face. He bit his lower lip, gazing at the running country through the window. Then he locked eyes with me.

"I'm a British spy trying to save my mate from the prison."

Whatever might have happened today, all the possibilities, I didn't expect this. The way he had said the word "mate" sounded strange. As if he had emphasized it on purpose.

"And you're telling me you're a British spy just like that, right?"

He nodded. "Yes."

"To me, huh? To the SS soldier?"

"Yes."

"Good joke, this one!"

"No. I don't believe you're an SS soldier."

"Why?"

He took a deep breath. "Look at you! You sat here with me. An SS soldier would hit me and drag me to his commander. You sat and talked to me. And you covered the door so no one would see us."

"It doesn't mean I'm not an SS soldier."

"No, it doesn't. But you're not an SS soldier."

I chuckled. This bloke was like from fairy tales. And quite naïve, too.

"I think you made up this story about being a British spy. So, who are you?" I said.

"My name is Alistair MacLeod. I'm a Secret Intelligence Service agent," he said in English and grinned, showing his teeth.

A Scotsman from MI6? His accent was different than I was used to when talking to the British I had occasionally met in Amsterdam, but the truth was that I'd never been to Scotland and never met any Scotsman.

He leaned closer and continued in English. "Have you ever heard about The Secret Intelligence Service?"

I nodded and spoke back in English. "Yes, MI6."

"Exactly!" He clasped his hands. "That's more proof you're not an SS soldier."

"How come?"

"They don't know our agency is called Military Intelligence, Section 6. Or MI6, for short."

A bunch of unclear memories flashed through my mind. Where had I heard that? Most likely from Anna when we'd talked about something.

"Why wouldn't they know it?" I said.

"Because the name is brand new." He grinned again and winked. "You're British like me. You speak English."

The faded memory took sharp contours. Yes, Anna was talking about it when we met at the cafe. It matched what this man had said. It was a brand-new name. No way! A real British spy right in front of me! I dared a small yet naïve test.

"Which Scottish city are you from? York?"

He chuckled. "York is English. North Yorkshire. I'm from the Scottish Highlands."

He had passed, and I tried to save the situation. "Oh, the Loch Ness Monster?"

His face hardened. "That's not a joke, all right? Stop it, or I make a wee hole into your heart." A baby Browning flashed in his hand. That got me. When had he managed to pull it out? And where from? He puckered his lips as if for a kiss and, at the same time, cocked the gun. *Incredible!*

We sat there, aiming guns at each other. I had a disadvantage: my submachine gun wasn't racked. The chamber was empty. I believed Alistair knew it. After a few seconds, he lowered the pistol. A big grin decorated his face again.

"Enough playing around, laddie. I could've killed you anytime, but I didn't, as you can see."

I said nothing but lowered the barrel, and my MP40 returned to its place on my back.

"Which organization you work for?" he said.

"I'm not working for Great Britain."

"Good. I don't care. You don't need to reveal it."

"What now?" I said.

"We should team up."

"What for?"

"You will help me to save the prisoner."

"I'm not sure…"

He interrupted me by waving his hand. "Enough games! I know you stopped the train before the British plane attacked. You have something to do with the bomb set in the SS headquarters. I saw you there, so please, don't try to hide it."

"There's nothing I want to hide."

His grin widened. "All right then. What's your answer to my offer?"

It sounded too good to be true. What would I get from it? An ally, at least. A helper. Although, if the Nazis had caught Alistair, my life would have been in danger. Alistair could've talked. They might have made him talk.

My face must have betrayed my thoughts.

"Don't hesitate, young man," he said. "We are on the same side. You're may not be from MI6, but we have the same queen. Don't forget that," he said, offering me his right hand.

I hesitated for a moment. *Ah, screw it!* I grabbed his hand, and we shook.

"So, what should I call you?" he said.

"Call me Max."

In my mind, I begged the universe not to give up on me.

"What's the plan?" Alistair said.

"I have no plan, so the question is: What's your plan?"

"We should get into the prison car and jump off the train with him."

"Easy to say, but impossible to do."

"Why? You're wearing their uniform."

"They are vigilant and aren't allowing anyone to enter the prison car."

Perhaps I just imagined it, but I thought I saw a relief blinking over his face. My concerns faded in an instant, though.

"We can shoot them," he said, mimicking shooting with his fingers.

I explained everything. The guards, their positions, the signaling. He nodded and dived into his thoughts, relaxing on the seat, and stretching his legs.

The train slowed down. I spotted a small town through the window. Or, as Alistair would say, a wee town. I glanced at him. He looked pretty relaxed. A real Highlander. He possessed a lot of the British stoicism, though. To my surprise, he pulled out a pipe and tobacco pouch. Despite the widespread stereotype, I'd never seen any British person smoke a pipe. They usually smoked cigarettes, just like the rest of the world.

The train stopped, and the sound of steps in heavy military boots boomed. A bunch of soldiers ran through the corridor. Alistair didn't give a shit. The pipe was more important. His hands, so deft with a gun, were less skilled when filling the pipe's bowl. More than half of the tobacco ended up on the seat and floor. He ignored the mess and reached for more tobacco from his pouch. I wasn't a smoker myself, but I knew he was wasting it, so I turned my attention to the station.

Then I spotted her. Sudden heat warmed my cheeks, and I couldn't prevent a sigh. My palm tapped the window without me controlling what I was doing. She was there, wearing her favorite red. Anna Bakker stood on the side of the platform in high heels. A cigarette stuck out of her lips. She put the lighter at the end and lit it. A cloud of smoke drifted up and dissolved in the open air.

"What?" Alistair said.

"There." I pointed my finger.

"Where?" He turned and gazed out in the direction I indicated.

"There. On the platform."

He slapped his thigh. "Come on, young man! I don't have horses to pull normal words out of you. What should I look at?"

"There. The woman in red. Can you see her?"

"That one?" He tapped on the window with the pipe's mouthpiece.

"Yes."

"Who is she?"

"She's my... boss."

"A boss?"

"It's complicated."

"All right. And?"

"She's here. It means she's following the train just as I asked her to. She can help us. I guess she brought some people."

"People?"

"People with guns. Warriors. Call them what you wish."

"The resistance?"

I said nothing, still gazing at her. She didn't try to spot me, find me in the crowd. She didn't need to. Her red dress was like a lighthouse. All she needed was to show herself. And she did exactly that. No more, no less. Accurate.

I jumped to my feet.

"What?" Alistair said.

"I must go out."

"To meet her?"

I ignored his question again and swung the coupe door open. "Meet you here in half an hour."

Alistair grinned and released a cloud. "At least you admitted you were here to free the prisoner."

Chapter 17

I ran across the platform to the front half of the train. It was already on the move as I rushed through the cars, scanning all the people's faces. Someone was here, I was sure of it. Or did I just hope someone would be here? Was it just my wish? No. Anna wouldn't have shown herself on the platform without purpose. She was up to something like she'd always been. Something that would move things forward. And I had to find out what it was. The resistance members could have boarded the train like everyone else, taking seats or standing in the aisles, ready to help me. Or hidden something in the dirty corners of a car. Under the seat, maybe. I had to find him. Or her. Or it.

The car was crowded. People pressed against each other, trying to hold onto whatever they could reach. A few just stood in the middle, held in place by the mass around them. No wonder. Adlerstein forbade all cars behind the prison car for ordinary passengers. My lungs protested as I breathed the heavy, smelly air while jostling forward.

People turned away from me when I looked at their faces. They were afraid. I pulled and pushed them, grabbing their sleeves, turning them, and checking every-one. It looked like I was searching for a new victim, for someone to be tortured and killed. Someone who had become an enemy of the regime. Fear yelled from their eyes, from their sweating skins. No one said a word, no one protested. They were broken. Already broken.

I wanted to cry out I wasn't the person who brought misery to their lives, but I couldn't. The uniform I wore was saying something different, and I had to keep things concealed. No one spoke up because nobody knew how many stool pigeons waited among the travelers. How many men or women who would profit from tipping off the SS or the gendarmerie? It was like being a mouse caught in a trap. Unable to escape but, at the same time, afraid to scream at the pain because it would lure the cat. And I was sick of all that comedy I had to play.

I passed two cars and nothing. No one stuck his head out, no one greeted me, at least, no one I would've known. In the third car, in the less crowded vestibule, I spotted a man with an enormous mustache. He could have been around forty years. His face was familiar. However, it didn't bring any specific memories. When our eyes locked, he turned away. I put my hand on his back, but he jerked and began to move forward, shouldering past people in his way.

"Wait!" I said, and the car vestibule went silent. Everyone stopped breathing. The tension became tangible.

The man reached for the door handle, but I grabbed him by his shoulder and forced him to turn. He was taller than me and wore a brown leather jacket.

"What do you want?" he said in broken German.

"Not here. Let's move somewhere else."

"I don't want to go. I did nothing wrong." His arms hung from his shoulders, dangling like two pieces of rope in a gentle breeze. The bloke's brows knit, and his lips pinched together.

"Don't worry," I said, grinning. His acting was great. "I won't harm you. I just need to talk."

"No." He jerked out of my grip. "You say you want just to talk, and I will never return. Let me be. I did nothing wrong."

"Sure, you did nothing wrong. Let's talk."

"No!"

He wanted to turn, but three or four pairs of hands grabbed him and held him on the spot. Other men standing behind him and to his sides stepped back, pressing more on each other, and creating a narrow space around me and the mustache man. Everyone acted as if I'd found a mass murderer who deserved to be judged on the spot and executed afterward. I suppressed the urge to yell at them, to ask what the hell they were doing. This man was one of them. They should protect him.

"He has something under his jacket," the man wearing small, round glasses said.

"Leave him be!" I said when he reached out and began to unbutton the other man's jacket.

The man with glasses didn't listen. He was eager to finish the task he'd given to himself. He wanted to serve the idiotic regime. To show he was a good citizen obeying the authorities. I couldn't believe what I saw.

I pushed him away. "What the fuck are you doing?"

A bar of chocolate fell to the floor from beneath the jacket, and the man with glasses picked it up, showing it to everyone. An excellent Belgian chocolate. I hadn't seen such a chocolate for a long time.

"See? I told you he was hiding something." His cheeks reddened with pride when he smirked.

With the gesture of a great hero who had just killed the monster that had terrorized the village, he handed me the chocolate. I smashed my fist right into his nose. The bloke squatted, pressing his palms to the spot of his wounded pride, and shrieking in agony. The blood smea-red around his nose as he was rubbing it.

People stared at me, confused, asking unspoken questions. No one dared to help that eager idiot. No one even dared to help the bloke with the mustache. I ignored them. Fear made them weak.

"Is there something you want to tell me?" I said, turning at the mustache man.

He shook his head.

I handed him the chocolate bar and moved forward, pushing him aside. He wasn't my man. He was just a bloke who happened to be in the wrong place. And this unnecessary theater had just made me sad. People moved out of my way, making room before the door to the aisle. I had no nerves for this. I would pass the rest of the cars, and if I didn't find a person or a message, I would get off the train at the next station. Enough of these dignity-killing scenes.

I opened the door to the aisle and stepped in. Like everywhere else, people sat on others' knees or stood in the aisle pressed on each other. When I passed the first three seats, someone touched my hand. I was startled, spinning to him. My blood pressure went down as quickly as it had risen. Jonas! I knew the bloke. From time to time, we met in Amsterdam bars. We'd never been close friends. Respected each other, though. He must have been my man. I cursed in my mind, calling myself names. Who else would Anna have sent if not a man I knew? I was such an idiot!

He pressed closer, handing me a piece of paper.

"You know what to do," he said and turned away from me, weaving his way toward the door.

The train stopped at the next station.

I locked myself in the toilet. My hands were shaking when I unfolded the piece of paper. It was a message from Anna. I recognized her writing style. She had always written in barely visible small letters.

"*We will attack the train after it passes Osnabrück. Use that moment to release the prisoner.*"

So, that was it. The plan was ready. I had to admit I didn't fancy it. They were risking their lives to help me. It was my idea to get on the train and try to free the spy. They should just follow the train, hidden, waiting for me to do everything. On the other hand, I was glad. I closed my eyes and sighed. My lips moved in silence, thanking the whole universe. I shouldn't be happy, I knew that. My dear friends could die because of me. I wasn't alone, though. That poured a new energy into my mind, poisoned with the experience of the last few hours.

I look at the piece of paper again. Where the hell was Osnabrück? Where was the train now, before or after this point? Practically speaking, the attack could start anytime from now. Yes, I'd gotten the message several minutes ago, but how long had Jonas been waiting for me?

What should I do now? At first sight, the attack seemed like a great idea if I ignored the risks they were taking. When the British plane had attacked, most of the soldiers were moved to the train's rear to help the machine guns. Nevertheless, passengers had been everywhere, blocking soldiers from securing firing positions. But that weakened the guards, leaving them without the support from off-duty soldiers. Now, it was different. The rear half of the train had no passengers. The soldiers could fire from anywhere, widening the impact of the defense. Even from the car where they were relaxing. I regretted that I hadn't burst into the prison car and shot the main guards when I was on duty with Stefan. When it had been easier to do. I could've already been miles away in safety. With the spy. With Anna and Simon. But now, I doubted I could do it alone.

If I could get rid of the signaling buzzer, that might help a lot. That wasn't possible, though. They had made it redundant. Cut the wire, and the buzzer would go off. Perhaps nobody would pay attention because they would be busy defending the train. I subconsciously shook my head. No. Too risky. What about having an accomplice and pretending I arrested him? I could pass the guards and go straight to the prison car. Risky. Less, but still risky. Feasible, though. I recalled the images of the cars and the guards and the prisoner. The plan wasn't so bad after all. I liked it more and more. It could be done. I imagined having coffee in Amsterdam's best cafe after this was over. Great. I just needed help.

I burned the message and threw the ash out through the window. The train was moving again. Opening the door, I stepped out. The crowded vestibule stank more than the toilet. People consumed all the oxygen. Their breaths warmed the air, and it caused their bodies, covered with too many layers of clothes, to sweat. The vestibule was too small for all the people who paid the fare to preserve their dignity. All because of one idiot who held the power to herd people as if they were livestock. I passed through the cars to the back until I reached the prison car, looking for Jonas, but with no success. Where the hell had that bloke gone? Right when I needed him. He must have gotten off the train when it waited in the station. Not good.

The thought I had suppressed previously appeared in a new light. Alistair. He was the only one who could help me.

Chapter 18

I found him hiding in the same coupe. He had drawn the curtains on the door. He was risking a lot. This was the only coupe in the car with drawn curtains. That could attract the attention of any soldier passing by. The man lay on the seat, his legs up, leaned against the wall. The sweet stench of sweaty fabric irritated my nose. It was like entering the locker room of a soccer team after a match. I opened the window and let the fresh air in.

"What?!" he said and set his feet on the floor.

"I can't breathe here."

"But why are you grinning like you found a million pounds?"

"I've got a good news."

"Hitler's dead, right?"

I chuckled. "That would be a fucking great news. I have only good news, though."

"So, tell me."

I explained to him the plan Anna and Simon had prepared. He listened, all ears, rubbing his chin and nodding.

"That's not bad. Really not bad. Where is Osnabrück?"

"I don't know."

"Interesting." His fingers sped up. I expected him to rub a hole into his chin.

"Do you like it?" I said, full of optimism.

The rubbing stopped, and he lifted his head. "No."

"Oh, for God's sake. Why not?"

"It makes no difference. You have to get into the prison car anyway. It doesn't make the danger any less."

"It does."

"How?"

"Now I can't get in, right? The guards, the guards at gangways, won't allow me. I tried it. Unless there's an officer with me."

"And?"

"They must be eliminated to get into the prison car, right?"

He nodded.

"But the car is open-spaced. There are almost no seats and no vestibules. So, it means a disadvantage in a shootout, right?"

He nodded again.

"On the other hand, the shootout could lure off-duty soldiers resting in the car behind either on the signaling or a noise from firing, right?"

"Yes, but…"

I interrupted him. "Wait! It looks like it is impossible to get there. But, when the plane attacked, all the soldiers got an order to gather at the back and fire on the plane. The guards were alone. No one would help them if anything happened."

"I'm not sure I'm getting it."

"Look, it's simple. Each soldier off duty fired at the plane. The car behind the guards was empty. Attacking the guards would be easy."

"But guards can set the alarm off."

"But there is no one to come, see?"

"Oh, I'm getting it. A false attack will create a distraction and move soldiers to the back. Like when the plane attacked." He rubbed his chin. "That's weak."

"Why weak?"

"No guarantee all soldiers would be moved."

"But most of them will."

He shook his head and relaxed, leaning over the seatback. His face said nothing about his thoughts.

"Come on! Listen carefully. I didn't finish. Getting to the prison car is possible, but I can't do it alone."

"Why?"

"Because I need someone to distract them, and then, when they won't expect it, I can kill them."

"And you didn't say it, but I expect I should be the distraction, right?"

"Yes!"

"How?"

"Perhaps we can pretend you're a new prisoner and I'm escorting you. It might even help to pass the rear guards without shooting."

Alistair lifted his legs on the seat and put his head between his knees, curling himself up. His breath slowed down like he was sleeping. I let him think. After a while, he raised his head.

"No, I don't like it."

"Why?"

"It puts me in danger. I won't have a gun."

"You do have one in your coat."

"I will be dead before I draw it out. Or they might pat me down and find it."

"Alistair, come on! We need to take some risk."

"Impossible! I need to know all the cards before I draw mine."

"Then you can lie back on the seat, crazy coward. This is about one of your mates. John Smith, remember? Why the hell are you so…" I swallowed the word. "…reluctant?"

He said nothing. His face didn't change. Bloody British. How could one communicate with them when they didn't express their thoughts and feelings?

"You almost danced with excitement when we met trying to convince me to shoot them, and now? Look at you!" I tried to motivate him, but nothing good came to my mind. Finally, I said, "Did that poor pilot die for nothing?"

He grinned. "That poor pilot died because he made a mistake. That's happening in the war, you know what I mean? Although, he didn't accomplish his task."

"What are you talking about?"

"His mission was to bomb the prison car and kill the agent."

My jaw dropped. "John Smith?"

He sighed. "The prisoner, all right?"

"Why the hell would he want to kill him?"

"He didn't want to. He had orders." He scratched his temple. "Oh, maybe he did, but no one will ever know because he's dead."

I frowned. "I'm lost."

"His orders were to kill John Smith because it's not John Smith." He leaned closer and whispered. "The prisoner is Sir Edmund Thorne."

My jaw dropped for the second time. "That British politician? The member of the war cabinet?"

Alistair nodded and crossed his arms over his chest, leaning back. He gazed at me like a spoiled child who had just revealed to his younger friend that Santa Claus didn't exist solely to torture him.

"You know that name?"

"Yes, from the newspapers, but…" I said, turning away from him. Now, everything made sense like never before. The British politician knew things hidden from the ordinary people. Even to the spies. I imagined what it could be. The strategy of the British defense. Secrets about air-force tactics. Plans for future battles. And many more. That would mean the end of the war. However, not the end people dreamed of. If Germany defeated Great Britain, Europe would be doomed. The Nazis would spread everywhere, and we wouldn't have the power to get rid of them. A few men and women would rather die fighting for freedom than live in terror. But most of us would adapt, as I saw some fifteen or twenty minutes ago. The apocalypse caused by mankind.

"Alistair, you MUST help me," I said in a low but firm voice. "Otherwise, we are all fucked."

He nodded. "I will, but we must craft a detailed plan and solve all known problems we can find."

"All right."

"Let's start with your suggestion that I be your prisoner."

"Go on."

He took the old newspaper laid on the seat and ripped off four pieces, laying them in a line.

"These are the cars with soldiers. The prisoner is in the middle. Two guards in each car. This is a car with off-duty soldiers, all right?"

I nodded.

He talked, pointing his finger from one paper scrap to another. I added my thoughts as well. We asked questions and found answers. We would try to fool the guards to get in. Then, we would use knives to eliminate the soldiers in the prison car. And jump out. No noise, nothing from the signalization. The B-plan was what I had suggested before: to shoot them all.

"Great. Looks good," Alistair said after minutes of discussion, tearing those four newspaper scraps into a million pieces.

"Let's move closer to the guards and prepare for the attack," I said and stood up.

"No. We need to wait."

"What for?"

"I must signal my people."

"What?!"

"Forget it. I shouldn't have mentioned it." He stood up and moved toward the door. "I'll meet you here in twenty minutes."

"But what if the attack begins?"

"It won't."

"How do you know that?"

"Look!" he said, pointing at the window. "The road is far away from the railroad. We can't see it because of the forest. They won't attack here, the forest will continue for a long time. We have a half an hour at least."

He was right. This stinking man who wore stinking old clothes was right. Everything went easier with him. He had a good nose for tactics and military thinking. With this man, the plan would succeed. The spy would be free, and the result of the war would be in the hands of soldiers once again and not in the hands of investigators and their torture. He was a member of a foreign secret service, though. I had to keep my mouth shut about certain things.

"See you there," he said and left.

The train slowed down, and after several minutes, stopped at the station. The label on the station building said Osnabrück.

Chapter 19

Two soldiers in their middle thirties sat on the seat, playing cards. I leaned against the vestibule door in the front of the car dedicated to the soldiers when off duty, observing them with their loud voices. Where were the others, I had no idea, and I didn't want to ask.

The train moved again. Twenty minutes had passed like nothing, and Alistair hadn't shown himself. I'd waited in the coupe, biting my nails and jumping all over the place. Every second had lasted longer than usual. I left the coupe and returned here. On my way, I'd bumped into several soldiers strolling up and down the train. It would have been suspicious if they had spotted me sitting in an empty coupe. Like I'd been slacking.

The country was changing. Gazing through the window, I could see the road. It ran along the railroad, both sides full of poplar trees. On the other side of the road, a field of corn stretched out to the horizon.

Not even the countryside's lovely look helped me focus on what was important. Things just went wrong. When the train stopped in Osnabrück, the soldiers forced passengers out of the train. All of them. New orders. Only soldiers were allowed to continue. And me. I hoped Alistair was hiding somewhere and no one had forced him to get off. The worst day of my life. Outside, my friends were preparing to attack the train while I was staring through the window, observing the field of corn. I had to change my plan. But how?

"Hey, *kamerad*! What's your name? Max, isn't it?" one soldier said.

"What?" I said and squinted at them.

"Come over and join us!"

"No. I don't like playing cards."

"Don't be stupid. Everyone likes playing cards."

"I'm not everyone." I turned back to the window.

One soldier stood up. "You think you're something special, huh?"

I said nothing and sat on the nearest seat, moving closer to the window. I wasn't in the mood for that stupid moron. He didn't understand that, though.

A hand yanked my shoulder. I gazed at him.

"I asked if you're something special. Did you hear that?"

"Leave me alone," I said and turned away.

He grabbed my shoulder again. "I asked you a question. It's polite to answer in the place where I'm from."

The vestibule door opened, and Stefan entered.

"Max, what's going on here?" he said.

"This young scumbag is impolite. Doesn't respect older men," the soldier said and reached out.

"Stefan, do you have a minute?" I said, ignoring the hand that was pulling me aside.

"Sure. Why?"

"Can we talk?"

"All right. Let's go somewhere else." He stepped forward, but the soldier blocked the aisle.

"First, this little scumbag must apologize to me and my friend," the soldier said.

"Leave us alone!" I said.

"Apologize!"

I jumped to my feet and stood close to him, smashing my fist right into his solar plexus. He released his grip, leaving his hand hanging in the air. His breathing stopped, and he bent forward. I grabbed his hands and spun him around, seating him in the place I'd occupied three seconds ago.

"Now we can go," I said to Stefan, and we moved through the aisle toward the back of the car.

The second soldier stared at me with his mouth open when we passed him by. He held the deck of cards with both hands. An interrupted shuffle. Two or three cards had already fallen on the dirty floor.

At the end of the aisle, I opened the door to the car vestibule and let Stefan pass. The second soldier jumped to his feet and ran to his friend, who was still sitting where I had put him. The punch into his abdomen had pacified him for a while. I doubted he would do anything for at least the next hour. Perhaps later, he would pour his anger over his friend, who was obviously less do-minant in their friendship. I didn't care. If they killed each other, I wouldn't mind.

The latch bolt clicked when I closed the door. The vestibule was dark and empty.

"What do you want?" Stefan said.

"Stefan, I'm in trouble and need help."

"All right, Max. How can I help you?"

I measured him from his feet to his head. Was he really my last chance? He wasn't a good soldier, but he could've understood why it would be the best thing to do. He didn't like the Nazi regime despite pretending to do so. I could use him as a distraction; no need for him to fire bullets. His moral values would stay untouched.

"Max?! How can I help you?"

"Stefan, first, everything we say here stays between us. Promise!"

"Of course, it will."

"Promise!"

"All right, I promise."

I took a deep breath. "Stefan, I'm not an SS soldier."

"What?!"

"I'm not an SS soldier. I disguised myself as one because I must free the prisoner."

"What?!"

"You understand very well, so please, make it easier for me and stop pretending you don't."

"But what does that have to do with me?" His eyes widened, and I could literally hear his heart pounding.

"I need you to help me to free the prisoner."

He stiffened.

I put my hand on his shoulder, feeling the tension in his body.

"Stefan, listen carefully. This is important. We need to free the prisoner. Otherwise, all of Europe will go to hell. Do you understand that? Everyone will be oppressed by the Nazi regime. Everyone."

His muscles released, and he shook his head slowly.

"We must save the prisoner from interrogation. He knows too much," I said.

His head was still moving from side to side.

"Stefan, help me, and I guarantee you will be free. I can get you out of the country. To Latin America or wherever you want to go."

He shook my hand off.

"Are you mad?!" His voice hissed. "Do you want to get me into trouble?"

"Stefan!"

"No!"

"Stefan!"

He stepped away from me, his face twitching.

"No! I can't do that. You don't know them. They won't kill me. They will torture me until I tell them what they want to hear. And at the end, I will beg them to kill me. And they will happily do it. Slowly."

He began to step backward until he bumped into the vestibule door.

"No. They won't kill me. They will do everything so that I will kill myself. And then they will laugh."

"Stefan, look at this from the other side. This is an opportunity to stop this madness."

"No, it's not! It's the one-way ticket to Prinz-Albrecht-Straße!" His hands trembled when he grabbed the cap on his head and put it down. "You can't imagine what they are capable of."

I gazed at him, observing his reactions. He waved with his cap, hitting the fingers of his other hand. His chest heaved, and beads of sweat dewed his forehead.

"Who are you, Max?" he said, rapidly blinking his eyes. His voice sounded high as if he were screaming and whispering at the same time. "Is your name even Max?"

"My name is not important. You can call me Max if you want. I'm a Dutch from Amsterdam. A private eye."

He slipped on the floor and tilted his head forward, leaning against the vestibule door.

"I can't do it even if I wanted to. Just can't."

"There's no one else left who can help me, Stefan. Only you."

"I'm sorry. I can't." He jumped on his feet. "Please, leave me alone. You have my word, I won't tell anyone. Just let me be. I can't."

He jumped to his feet and pushed me slightly aside, then opened the door leading to the gangway. Last gaze at my eyes. Last shaking of his head.

"I can't."

He left, slamming the door behind him.

What now? The chances of finishing the task were low. Alistair had disappeared. Stefan shitted his pants. Me alone attacking the guard meant I would be killed in seconds.

The countryside flickered behind the stained window on the door. A truck appeared in the turn. Its roof door was opened, and a man stuck himself out. I didn't recognize his face, but I was sure it was Simon. Yes, he put his hat down, and the movement of his hand was typical for him.

Simon pulled the machine gun from the truck's inside and unfolded the bipod, securing it on the truck's roof.

I had to do it myself. I had to take the risk. There were no other options. I would pretend someone sent me to do something. Or just pass to the front of the train with an order. That was a great idea. Just pass, not having anything to do with the prisoner. That would distract them. This car was empty, not counting those two play-ing cards. All the soldiers were somewhere else. The guards weakened. In the worst case, I would shoot the prisoner if there was no other option. Perhaps I would die. I tried to convince myself that I didn't give a shit. But I did.

Chapter 20

Hauptsturmführer Emil Hartmann Adlerstein smoothed the wrinkles on his trousers and checked whether all buttons on his uniform jacket were fastened. His skin got goosebumps as he shivered from inside. Wearing this uniform designed by Karl Diebitsch and Walter Heck, two sons of the great German nation, was a privilege not many people understood. He liked the gentle touch of its soft fabric. All things were moving easily like a hot knife through butter. Just a few more hours and the train would stop at *Anhalter Bahnhof* in Berlin. His super-intendents would be surprised. And he would finally earn what he and his ancestors had deserved for centuries.

He touched the sword secured to his belt. The handle was cold but convenient. All the officers in Berlin laug-hed at him for the sword. They didn't understand the importance of his heritage. Memories flashed through his mind. His father had forced him to practice fencing every day. His limbs had hurt endlessly after every session. The officers laughed, but now, it would be him who would deliver *two* British prisoners instead of the one they had already had in captivity. The British would suffer. Unbelievable how easily he could've outfoxed that mo-ron, the second British agent he had met. The bloke had been so stupid, telling everything about the attack. Adlerstein congratulated himself for being wise and doubled the soldiers guarding the agent. Now, he didn't need to worry about the prisoner. Even if the second agent tried something, they would overpower him. And the rest of the soldiers could focus on the upcoming attack. He would deal with that British moron later.

Adlerstein left his coupe and headed toward the end of the train. On his way, he checked on the soldiers spread along the last four cars of the train and whether they were ready to fire. Everything was all right. Each soldier was in his position. Good. He opened the door and passed through the gangway, entering the last car. The strong draft from opened rolling doors welcomed him. The commanding officer, *Untersturmführer* Klein, saluted and gave him a short briefing, during which he stared at the sword. That pumped Adlerstein's blood pressure. *An idiot.*

"Enough!" Adlerstein said, interrupting him. He had to speak up to drown out the rumble of the wheel on the rails. He had to keep the rolling doors open, though.

The machine guns stood at their spots, covered by sandbags. The gunners lay behind them and looked tired, especially the one whose left eyelid was red and swollen.

"What happened to your eye, soldier?"

The gunner twisted and got on all fours.

"Don't stand up. Just tell me what happened."

"I stared too long to the sun when I was firing, *Herr Hauptsturmführer.*"

"*Untersturmführer*, replace this man! Can't you see he's not able to operate the gun? How will he aim with a swollen eye?"

"*Jawohl, Herr Hauptsturmführer.*" He clacked his heels.

"If you fuck up, I'm going to hang you on the nearest tree, *verstehen Sie*?"

"*Jawohl, Herr Hauptsturmführer.*" He clacked his heels again, his hand forgotten, stretching in the air.

Untersturmführer's face revealed how he hated Adlerstein for scolding him in front of low-ranking officers and privates, but it also revealed he was afraid to oppose him. That was right. Fear was the best tool to keep them all focused. Every single soldier had to understand the importance of this mission. Adlerstein's mission. Mercy had no place in the war. *I will kill everyone who will ruin it. Everyone!*

"So, don't wait for someone else to do it instead of you and act!"

The *Untersturmführer* stopped saluting and spun. He pointed at one soldier.

"Tischbein, take his position! You will be a gunner from now on!"

The soldiers changed their posts.

"You! What's your name?" Adlerstein pointed at the soldier with the swollen eye.

"*Sturmmann* Fischer, *Herr Hauptsturmführer!*"

"*Sturmmann* Fischer, go to the corner and lie on the floor. You're allowed to smoke and take a nap!"

"*Jawohl, Herr Hauptsturmführer.* Thank you, *Herr Hauptsturmführer.*" The soldier turned and sat in the corner, leaning against the walls.

And those who served with honesty and were loyal, he would reward generously. Like this soldier. He deserved his rest. But if his eye didn't get better soon, he would send him away. Adlerstein didn't need cripples in his army. His army. How magnificent that sounded.

"Do you have sufficient ammunition?" he said, turning at *Untersturmführer.*

"Yes, *Herr Hauptsturmführer.* We got extra boxes from the *Wehrmacht* at one station."

Adlerstein nodded. "Good. Another attack is going to happen soon. This time, it will be a ground attack."

He scanned the machine guns. They covered a wide traverse angle, but the back of the train was open to potential attackers.

"Move one MG 42 to the rear gangway!"

"With all due respect, *Herr Hauptsturmführer*, it's impossible."

Adlerstein frowned, shooting daggers at him. *Untersturmführer* lowered under his sight.

"I hate the words 'not possible'," he said in a low, threatening voice, clenching his teeth.

"The gangway is narrow, as is the door. The gunner will lose the arc of fire."

"Do as I say and move this machine gun to the gangway!" Adlerstein pointed at the weapon on his right side.

Untersturmführer gave an order to two men. They retracted the machine gun's bipod and shifted the heavy weapon. The narrow door frame forced them to unfold the bipod outside. But the gun's body was too long. The gunner shook his head when he laid on the floor and gripped the handle. He fidgeted, trying to find the best position. The door's threshold pressed against his belly. After a while, he rolled to the side, casting a questioning face.

"Move it a bit inside!" Adlerstein said.

They did. The gunner's operating space improved, although the gun didn't cover the entire angle. It was sufficient for Adlerstein.

"Next time," he said to *Untersturmführer*, "if you don't obey my order immediately, I will shoot you in the face."

The man swallowed, clipping with his eyelids.

"Keep your eyes on the road. I'll stay here and lead the defense myself."

"*Jawohl, Herr Hauptsturmführer.*"

An intense sensation of satisfaction poured through his entire body. He was the best commander in the army. He had the prerequisites for that. His family had been fighting in wars for the last couple of centuries. The pride locked his chest, making it difficult to take a breath.

"A truck on the road!" *Untersturmführer* said.

Adlerstein felt a strong urge to kick him. That moron dared to warn for what was obvious. *Fucking toady.*

The truck slowed down and appeared behind the train. A man stood up through the truck's roof, firing a round at them. It caused no harm. The bullets hit railroad ties or just flew uselessly through the air. Adlerstein grinned. He knew his calculations had been correct. The truck was an easy target for the machine gun in the new position. The level of testosterone rose.

"*Feuer frei!* Fire at will!"

The gunner in the new position fired, but bullets pierced the gangway's wooden floor. The train was too high above the road. The gunner had a negative inclination angle.

Adlerstein looked around, seeking something they could put under the bipod to level the machine gun. A few more bullets chipped the wooden floor. All faces gazed at him in panic. The gunner lay on the floor cold dead.

I opened the gangway door to the car with rear guards and stood still. The clack of slides sent an aggressive welcome. Four soldiers aimed their guns at me.

"What the hell are you doing here, *kamerad*?!" the old soldier said, and they all tilted their MP40s down.

"What?" I said.

I closed the door and strode toward them. Four soldiers, what did that mean? It wasn't the guard exchange time. Another change I hadn't foreseen?

"You should be helping the machine guns. Something is going on here," the old soldier said when I got closer.

"What is it?"

"No one knows. The commander keeps his secrets well hidden." They chuckled.

"No, seriously, what is happening?"

"Where were you when new orders arrived?"

I said nothing.

"You were sleeping, right, *kamerad*?" another soldier said.

"Yes, I was. Please, don't tell anyone," I said, casting the face of a scared rabbit, and added, "*Kamerad*."

He waved his hand. "Don't worry. No one cared."

"And what are the new orders?"

"They doubled the guards. And the rest went to the back of the train. Looks like another plane attack."

"Oh, those orders? I thought something bad happened."

"Isn't that bad enough?" the old soldier said.

"It is. I thought of something else. Anyway, I have a message for the guard commander. From *Hauptsturmführer* Adlerstein. Let me pass."

I moved forward, but the old soldier put his hand on my chest.

"Don't need to rush, young man. The guard commander is in the car behind you."

"No, he isn't."

"Oh, yeah, he is."

"I just came from there. They told me he went to the mail car."

"Who told you that?"

"A soldier."

"And his name was?"

"Bingo was his name." I shrugged. "Should I remember every name? I don't know even your name."

He measured me from head to foot. I grinned at him as if he was my long-time-known buddy.

"No. I think you should go back."

"Come on! I must deliver the message!"

He leaned closer to me. "But I don't believe you."

"I will tell him you stopped me from doing my duty."

"To whom?"

"*Hauptsturmführer* Adlerstein."

"You can. I don't give a shit."

The three other soldiers chuckled.

He stood there like a king who had just refused pilgrims crossing his land and waited for their reaction. What could I do? Their guns were ready to send me straight to hell.

"Look, *kameraden*!" the bloke with a shaved face said, pointing at the window.

Outside, the truck driver adjusted the truck to the train's speed. Simon fired. The flames from the machine gun flashed from the shadow of his body. Everyone, except me and the old soldier, stepped closer to the window, forgetting what they were here for.

"*Mein Gott*, the British are attacking again!"

"Look how aggressive they are."

"We have their man. Wouldn't you be aggressive?"

The old soldier turned at me. "You should go to the back and help others, young man."

The truck left the paved road and got closer to the train, bouncing on the gravel surface. Simon showered the train with more bullets.

"Look at them! They are crazy!"

"Our gunners will get them, don't worry. Like they did to the British plane."

"Go!" the old soldier said, pointing at the door. He turned to the window.

No time to wait for something to happen. I had to act now. The slide on my MP40 clacked when I racked it. My finger didn't pull the trigger, though. I felt a sudden weakness in my entire arm and fought with a spasm. *What the hell is wrong with me?!*

They spun in an instant. All guns were aiming at me again, ready to put holes through my body if I moved. A familiar face gazed at me. Now, I recognized him. The *Oberschütze* I had been in the mail car with. This was his moment. His eyes sent the message, *"See? You shouldn't have messed with me!"*

"Don't do that, son," the old soldier said. "I don't want to kill you."

"I need to deliver a message, all right?"

"You need to return and help the others."

My gun aimed at them, and they aimed at me. Whatever I did, I would be dead in seconds. I could kill two or maybe three of them. The prisoner would be still in captivity, though. There was nothing I could hide behind. No seats around, no partitions. The only seats at the end of the car were too far away to help in this situation.

I began to step backward. They spread out in a line in front of the gangway door. Their eyes locked on me. I felt their gazes reading my mind and waiting for the signal to fire.

The old soldier nodded. "Good. Slowly. I don't want to kill you, but I won't let you harm me or my boys."

"Your boys? You're not their father. You're a private like me or them," I said.

"It doesn't matter. They are my boys."

The others nodded and huddled closer together. One move of my hands, and I could get them all. One move and a jump behind the seat. A few more steps.

I caught a glimpse of the seats at the end of the car. My heartbeat calmed. I breathed freely. My vision sharpened. There was just me and them. Everything else faded out. The moment came.

I pulled the trigger and swept my hand in a circle. Half a second later, I jumped between the seats on my right side. The bullets made holes in the wall. I spotted them when I flew through the air. I missed. All of them.

The soldiers didn't hesitate and began to play the deadly symphony of the MP40s. The seatback above my head tore apart. Bullets pierced through it like it was paper. After five seconds, the concert stopped.

"Are you still alive?!" the old soldier said.

"No. I'm on my way to heaven!" I said.

I couldn't see their legs. The metal box fixed beneath the seat blocked my vision. My mistake. I should've jumped to the left. I could've had a perfect line to shoot their feet. The metal box covered me, though.

"Now, son. I will forgive you for your stupidity and let you go. Toss your gun out so I can see it, and you can go."

"And you'll shoot me in the back. Forget it," I said.

"You have my word we won't shoot. But your gun must stay here."

I said nothing. There was nothing to say.

"I promise I won't even tell about this incident. None of us will, right, boys?"

"Yes. Yes," the voices said almost as one.

"I've heard such promises many times."

They whispered something. I heard their murmur des-pite the rumbling wheels of the car.

The old soldier's voice echoed. "I'm coming to you!"

I spun and glanced back. The back door was around eight or ten feet from me. Running straight toward it would be madness. But madness was exactly what I needed. I could've jumped from side to side and fired at them.

The floor vibrated slightly under the weight of his steps. I peered from behind the metal box. He was fifteen or twenty feet from me. I saw his legs. He took small steps, tiptoeing. I didn't understand why.

I stuck out the submachine gun into the aisle and pulled the trigger. The gun barked and sent a short batch of bullets. Something tumbled to the floor.

"You little prick! You killed him!" That was the last thing I heard before the second round began. Bullets flew above me. The metal box clanged every time a bullet found its way to it. I thanked the universe for my first decision to hide on this side of the aisle, admitting my previous wish was stupid. No more regrets. Each of those bullets would've poked a crimson hole in my skin.

I kept my hand in the aisle, aiming blindly and firing until the mag went empty. Ready to change it, I reached down and pulled another mag from the pouch on my belt.

Shit! The slide wasn't pulled back. It wasn't an empty mag. The casing had jammed, blocking the slide from pushing it into the chamber. I yanked it several times, but it didn't move. Useless piece of metal crap. I smashed the submachine gun on the floor. It didn't help.

The shooting stopped. I slid on the floor, peering from behind the metal box.

All the soldiers were changing their mags. They had made the rookie mistake of desynchronization.

My body sprang, and I flew toward the back gangway, taking giant leaps like a deer running for its life. My mind focused solely on the door. The rumbling of the car disappeared.

The metallic clack of the slide thundered. It pierced through my mind.

Two leaps. Half a second of my life. Quite shitty, though.

I grabbed the door handle and yanked the door wide, jumping through it and sliding aside behind the wall. The fresh air touched my face.

The door slammed, and several bullets pierced it. Staying here was a bad idea. I needed to move further. I took a deep breath as if it was going to be my last one.

Chapter 21

I crawled through the gangway and got into the next car. Daring to stand up and peering through the door win-dow, I checked the situation inside, expecting two or three soldiers to be relaxing after duty. The car was empty, though. I entered. Adlerstein must have moved all the soldiers to the back of the train. Just like the old soldier had said. What now?

I heard a muted sound behind me and glanced back through the door window. The soldiers rattled the pierced door. One or two bullets had hit the lock, and it got stuck. They must have kicked it a few times. That was what I'd heard. In this case, kicking wouldn't help. The door opened to the inside, not outside. I glanced around, looking for something I could use to block this door. Nothing. Running away was the first option that came to my mind. But where? To the end of the train? Blending in with the other soldiers? Not possible. My disguise was exposed. Jumping off the train was a bad idea, too. They would see me and fire after me. I would become a target. I had to hide. The rattling increased, and the door gave up. They got through.

I ran along the aisle and entered the next car. It had a vestibule. I passed the toilet. Barely stopping, I opened it and slipped in right when I heard the gangway door open. The door bolt clicked when I slid it. The bathroom was small and dark because the glass on the window was painted over. The walls were made of wood, as was the door. Despite the thickness of the massive door, bullets from MP40 would eat through it like a cream dessert. I was sure the soldiers saw me getting here. I opened the awning window. It slanted a bit but didn't open wide. Not my way out. Two metallic handles were mounted to the ceiling. Men used them when urinating to eliminate the shocks from the shaking car. I grabbed them and pulled my body up, fixing my legs against the wall above the door frame and praying the soldiers wouldn't aim up.

The door's handle fluttered.

"Open! Open, you fucker!"

Somebody kicked the door. It boomed like thunder, but the door didn't open. The narrow space amplified the sounds in a bizarre way.

The muscles in my arms began to get tired. My lungs craved oxygen and made my breathing faster. The sweat covered my forehead and flowed down under gravity. My back was soaked. The handles became slippery. I tensed my legs, pulling more against the wall, and lifted my belly so it touched the ceiling. It eased the pressure on my hands a bit.

Slides clacked.

"Last chance to surrender!"

My palms began to slide slowly from the handles.

The submachine guns barked. Chips and dust filled the narrow space. Bullets sought their way out, making a sieve of the door and shattering the half-opened window into a million shards. My lungs refused to breathe the dusty air, forcing me to cough. The shooting deafened my ears.

Suddenly, both handles tore away from the screws under my weight, and I fell to the floor. At the same moment, a bullet sliced my arm.

The soldiers emptied their mags. The silence cut deep into my deafened ears. It hurt. Three seconds, and no-thing. Then, someone kicked the door open. The hinges cried, and, squealing, the door fell on me, hitting my nose hard. The sharp pain spread down to my feet. I couldn't move, even if I had wanted to. Only my wounded arm stuck from beneath the door, gushing blood.

"There you are, stupid moron! Dead as deserved," one voice said.

"Is he really dead?" another voice said.

I held my breath.

Someone stamped on the door. I tensed all my muscles, swallowing the scream that wanted to erupt out of my lungs.

"He's dead."

"I don't believe it."

"Look, he's bleeding."

"From his arm."

"If he bleeds from his arm, he must be bleeding from his chest or belly as well."

"That's stupid!"

"Pull the door up and check it with your eyes."

"I won't do that."

"Why?"

"What if he's dead? I don't want to see his dead face."

"Then shoot another round."

"I have no bullets."

"Me neither."

"We should return."

"Yeah, he's definitely dead." The same soldier, I guessed it was him, stamped again on the door, pumping with his leg. I clenched my teeth, holding my breath. My body was one solid spasm.

"See, I told you. He would cry if he were alive."

"I'll come here later and check if he's still here."

"That's your problem. I don't care. To me, he's dead, and that's what I'm going to report."

Their steps rumbled away from me. A door slammed in the distance. I waited a few more minutes, thanking the universe and all the gods that appeared throughout human history. I was a lucky bastard and didn't know why I deserved it. Lifting the door a bit, I slipped from beneath it. They had aimed mostly at the same place. If I hadn't pulled myself up, I would've received the first dose of bullets right to my chest.

Everything was ruined. I couldn't use my disguise anymore. My arm was bleeding. I had no hope. I had no gun. I'd left it there. It was useless, anyway. There was nothing that would keep me on this train anymore. I'd had enough. The only thing I could think about was jumping off at the first opportunity. To leave this difficult space. I'd done what I could.

But first, I had to signal to Simon to stop and back off the fight. This madness must have stopped. Now. It reached its end.

The shattered window provided a good view of the truck. My heart burst with joy. Whoever was driving the truck was smart and knew what he was doing. He kept it behind the train. Away from the arc of fire of the machine guns. On the contrary, Simon had an open space . He could shoot and kill everyone in the machine gun car, but that was not the goal of this action. The flames didn't flare often from the barrel. The right time to back off.

I stuck my hand through the window and waved at them. No response. I put my jacket down and stuck it through the window, waving like crazy. Nothing. No reaction. I needed something bigger. Something that could attract their attention. My eyes landed on the door. Without thinking, I bent and lifted the heavy piece of wood. No one would need it. My wounded arm pro-tested, but the adrenaline rush silenced everything.

Huffing and puffing, I leaned the door's edge against the window's border. *Shit!* The door was wider than the opening, it didn't fit through. I threw it to the floor. It rumbled. This was all Alistair's fault. Where the hell was he? He'd promised to help and then disappeared. Perhaps, before leaving, I should've found him and kick his ass. I stepped next to the hole that had once been a window and peered out. The truck still kept a safe distance behind the train. Should I jump now? Simon and the others didn't seem to be in danger.

The railroad bent in a long arc. I could see the cars at the back and the barrels of machine guns hidden behind the sandbag emplacement. They fired. A few soldiers fired through opened windows in other passenger cars.

The truck sped up. No. The train slowed down. The arc of the railroad caused the last car to stay in sight of the truck. That created a better firing line for the Nazis, opening the arc of fire more. Bullets showered the road dangerously close to the truck, making dust clouds on the ground and mowing the grass around the road.

And then, the truck wobbled from side to side. Those bastards shot the tire on the left front wheel. I saw the rubber shredding as it spun. Simon had to hold the wheel with both hands. The released machine gun flew away, doing somersaults and bouncing on the gravel road. The ammunition belt snaked through the air like a dark rib-bon. The truck went off the road, hiding behind the dense stripe of trees. I stood there breathless, waiting for the vehicle to appear somewhere. It had to appear somewhere. I needed to know they were all right.

The flames from the blast burned in a red-yellow ball above the trees, leaving a cloud of dark smoke rising to the sky. The truck had exploded. I knew it, although I spotted only the flames. What else could've possibly created such a giant fireball?

The shattering soreness scattered over my chest. I spat out a mouthful of bitter saliva. No, this couldn't be true. It just couldn't. But I'd seen it. I tried to wipe my eyes, but my hands were too heavy. I'd seen it. The truck had exploded. Simon was dead. And the others had died with him. Anna, had she been there? I couldn't recall the image of the truck on the road. My throat tightened, and I felt my heart pulsing in it. This was the end. Nothing mattered anymore.

Chapter 22

I hid in the last coupe of the first passenger car of the train. My arm was bleeding, and I wanted to put something on it before I jumped off the train. Spending time on the gangway, I had found a way to avoid passing through the cars with the guards and the prisoner. It wasn't comfortable, though. I'd climbed the ladder mounted at each gangway, crawled over the roof, and descended the other gangway. The air stream worked against me, but on all fours, it was more straightforward than I thought. The worst part was checking to see if the guards had been watching through the door window. I made it up to the first passenger car, though. I'd met a few soldiers, but the news about me hadn't spread yet, I guessed.

I tore off the back of my shirt and created a provisional dressing. Nothing extra special, but it would stop bleeding or slow it down. It protected the wound from infection, too. I wiped off the fresh blood. Simon was dead! The man who had once saved my life was dead! Sorrow clouded my mind again. I tried to shut out the entire world, but images kept returning again and again. The prisoner. The truck with Simon sticking from the roof. The fireball. The coupe's walls collapsed on me.

The door opened, and Alistair stepped in. He took a seat in front of me. What the heck?! He wore a Nazi uniform! I tilted my head down, ignoring him. How the hell had he found me here?

"So, it didn't go well," he said after minutes of silence.

I said nothing.

"I'm sorry I couldn't be there."

My head still faced my boots.

He leaned forward and grabbed my shoulders, straightening my neck. "I couldn't help, do you understand?"

I gazed at him. My inner daemon told me to strangle him with his own belt. Then, fix the belt outside the car and let his dead body wave in the air stream like a flag until it was torn into micro-pieces and spread over the country. But I didn't. Alistair MacLeod meant dust to me. He was less than a morning fart.

"Say something!"

"What are you wearing?" I said in a low voice and shook his hands off my shoulders.

"This?" he dusted off his jacket. "This is my disguise. Same as yours. I just managed to get an officer's uniform."

"You're a piece of shit, Alistair."

He sighed. "I know."

"You're a piece of shit. Good people died because of you."

"I know." He sighed. "Maybe you didn't notice, but there's a war going on. People are dying."

"And what now? You will sit here and repeat your 'I know.' Is that supposed to help me?!"

His eyes widened as my voice rose.

"Fuck you, Alistair!"

"You don't understand."

"I don't understand what?! You promised you would be there."

"I'm sorry," he said in a low sad voice.

"Fuck you and your 'I'm sorry'!"

"I had to do an important thing. Very important. I'm sorry that it took so long and made me miss the attack."

"Now you feel sorry? Do you think it will bring them back?"

"No, I don't think it will."

"Tell me one thing, Alistair. Are you doing this on purpose?"

"Doing what?"

"Sabotaging everything."

"I have my orders, and my orders are more important than you and your mates. I told you that already."

"Your orders were to prevent the spy from being interrogated, right?"

He nodded. "Yes, that's right."

"But now, now you can watch how the best torturers of the fucking German Reich will pull, word by word, all secret information and change the history of mankind forever!"

Saying that drained all my energy. I fell against the seatback. Alistair said nothing.

"It's over, Alistair. Over."

"No, that's not true."

"Oh, really?"

"Yes. And I'll prove it to you."

"How?"

His body sprang. "I'm going to free the prisoner with you. Now," he said, gesturing with his hands.

"Don't bother. Everything is in deep shit."

"No. You just don't understand what is happening. There's no time for hesitation. In two hours, the train will arrive in Berlin. We have to act now."

"I don't care!"

"Head up, soldier!"

"I'm not a soldier."

"Yes, you are. You wear a uniform."

"No!" I spat on the floor. "This is what I think about this uniform."

He said nothing, locking eyes with me. His face was like stone. Like a cold, bloody, emotionless stone. I didn't care any longer for him or his orders and intentions. My role in this tragedy had ended when the bullet scratched my arm, and the truck exploded.

"I'm going to jump off this cursed train as soon as possible," I said.

"No, you won't."

"Watch and learn."

Alistair lifted his finger.

"Now, pay attention, young man. Here's the plan. I will escort you to the prison car."

"And?"

"And we will pretend I have found you and caught you."

"And?"

"Then we will shoot the guards and jump off with the prisoner."

"That's stupid!"

"You suggested the same scenario, do you remember?"

My blood pressure rocketed. I moved off the seatback, straightening my upper body. "That was different, don't you think? I had support from the out-side."

"But now, I have a Nazi uniform, and you are a man… Well, everyone is seeking you. You are the most wanted man on this train."

"How do you know that?"

"I have ears, and I listen."

"Fuck you and your plan as well," I said and turned my face to the window.

"That doesn't sound like you."

"I don't give a shit how it sounds."

His hand moved, reaching for his belt, and the barrel of a gun yawned at me. I leaned against the seatback again, ignoring him. It wasn't the first barrel pointed at me today. It just didn't bother me anymore.

"You will go, and you will go now!" Alistair said.

I crossed my legs, grinning at him and fidgeting on the seat to find the most comfortable position.

"I mean it!" he said.

I began to whistle the Lili Marleen song.

"Come on!" Alistair's face wrinkled. He was losing ground under his feet.

"I see you got the uniform with a Walther in one package. Where's your Baby Browning?"

He said nothing.

I grabbed his hand and moved it up, so now the barrel pointed at my forehead. "You must kill me, Alistair. That's the only way you can get me into the prison car," I said.

"You know I won't do that." He jerked his hand from my grip and pointed the pistol down. "Look, I guarantee you will receive the highest award possible. You'll get a medal, young man."

"Alistair, know you what?" I leaned closer.

"What?" He leaned as well.

I whispered, "Take your medal and stick it up to your ass."

He leaned back. "You're a moron."

I couldn't any longer listen to this idiot, so I stood and grabbed the door handle.

"I knew you would do it!" he said and stood as well.

"You're mistaken. I'm going to jump off the train. Now."

I opened the door ajar and peered out. The corridor was empty. With no hesitation, I left the coupe. Alistair followed.

"You can't jump off the train just like that!"

"Watch and learn," I said the old boring phrase again.

Turning behind the corridor's corner, I stiffened. The many faces of people in uniform waited there. Hands ro-cketed into the air, grabbing me wherever they could and pulling me forward with such strength as if a pair of horses pulled me. Before I could say 'hello,' I was thrown down. The soldiers pressed on my limbs with their hands and knees, pushing my face against the dirty floor.

"We got him, *Herr Hauptsturmführer*," said one soldier in German.

"Great," Alistair said in the same language. "Turn him so I can talk to him."

They obeyed, and I was facing the Nazi officer uniform again. This time, I knew it was the last officer uniform I was going to see.

Chapter 23

"So, what a pleasant change of the situation, isn't it?" he said in German.

I turned my head away from him, saying nothing.

"And now, you decided to be quiet?"

I kept my silence. Many questions swirled in my head. I was confused, and before I would do anything, I needed to think about what had just happened. Had this moron been with the Nazis all the time, or had he just changed sides? They took everything that I could've used to harm them. Even the knife hidden in my boot.

"You're not getting it, are you?" he said.

A ruthless smirk sat on his face. His eyes threw lightning. He stepped closer and kicked me.

"Will you talk?"

"Sod off, Alistair, or whoever you are," I said in a low voice.

The soldiers chuckled but stopped when his stern gaze lit on them. He pointed his finger at me and nodded. One soldier punched my wounded arm. The sharp pain blasted through my consciousness, leaving my limbs numb. I clenched my teeth. This son of the bitch didn't deserve to see my pain.

"Oh, a hero." he grinned again. "Let's see what kind of suffering will open his mouth. *Rottenführer*, stretch his hand as far as possible!"

The asked soldier didn't hesitate and pulled my wounded arm while the rest nailed my body to the floor. The pain from the stretched wound was unbearable. The darkness spread in my brain, weakening my resistance. I lost vision. All my senses focused on the pain. I gathered the remainder of my strength, trying to block an ima-ginary knife cutting through me. I felt the moistness of the blood running from behind the temporary dressing.

Alistair bent and poked his dirty finger into the dressing covering my wound. I couldn't make it. My lungs opened, and the wild scream popped out right to his face. The soldier stopped pulling.

"Do you feel any better now?" Alistair said and straightened.

"Sure," I said, pushing each word through my clenched teeth. "Better than ten doctors."

"I can repeat that if you like."

"Go to hell, dirty Nazi fucker!"

Alistair shook his head. "It looks like Mr. British agent is still not getting it. *Rottenführer*, next round!"

The torture repeated. This time, I didn't try to block it. My lungs filled with air, and I let the scream out. The pulling stopped in an instant. My head spun, and hazy sparks danced before my eyes. Beads of sweat wet my forehead. The scream changed its direction to a huge air intake. Oxygen. I needed more oxygen.

I felt the tension in my wounded arm. That moron was about to pull it again.

"All right, I will speak!"

Alistair waved his arm, drawing the soldiers' attention. "This is exactly what a very good friend of mine, Doctor Josef Mengele, taught me. Make him scream, and he will happily reveal all his secrets." He turned back to me, grinning as if he had just disarmed a ticking bomb. So, can we finally talk like adult men?"

"What do you want to talk about?" I said, gasping.

"First of all, tell me who's your commander."

"I have no commander."

"Really? So, the plane attack, stopping the train, and the ground attack were just your child's play, right?" He spread his arms. "One day, you woke up and decided to mess with me."

The soldiers chuckled but didn't stop pressing me to the floor.

"Alistair, I have no idea what you are talking about. I didn't stop the train."

"Alistair? You still believe I'm Alistair?" He shifted his sight to the soldiers, and they all laughed.

"You!" He pointed at one soldier. "Tell him who I am!"

"He is *Hauptsturmführer* Adlerstein, you idiot!" the soldier said.

A hot wave of embarrassment flew through my veins. Stupid, stupid, stupid. How could this moron have fooled me with such a simple trick? He had been pulling my leg all the time! And I revealed everything to him. Every-thing? I remembered not telling the names and where the people were from, though.

"You're an idiot," I said in a low voice, trying to spit out my shame.

He shook his head. "No. You're an idiot. It was you all the time. I played with you. And you? You were the idiot who let himself be manipulated. Tie him and take him back to the coupe!"

The soldiers must have been ready for this because they had already prepared chunks of rope. A few hands held me while the rest bound my legs and arms. As they twisted my arms behind my back, I jerked from the sudden pain in my wounded arm.

"Be careful with him!" Adlerstein said, "So the big boy won't complain."

His comment caused a burst of laughter among the soldiers, but the pressure weakened. Despite having my arms tied behind my back, I could move them. The image of me moving my arms forward over my legs flashed in my mind.

"Now, fasten those leather belts around his body! He's an idiot, but he will not give up easily. I see on his face that the bird would like to leave the cage."

They did as they were told, and then, carrying me like a coffin at a funeral, they brought me to the coupe I left several minutes ago. I ended up sitting on the seat and leaning against the window wall. No way to run away. Not even if I wanted to. I had to figure out what he knew, what I had spilled. The soldiers left, and Adlerstein stepped in, closing the coupe door behind him.

"Now, British agent, tell me your name and the name of your commander," Adlerstein said and installed himself on the opposite seat.

"I'm not a British agent."

"I asked you to tell the names! Not to admit you're a British agent."

"Maximilian Müller. That's my name."

"No, it isn't. Your German is excellent, but you're not German. And Maximilian Müller is a German name."

"I've never said I was German. I was born to German parents and grew up in Amsterdam," I said.

"That's a lie, but go on!"

"I am a member of the German resistance in Berlin."

He rubbed his chin. "Interesting."

"Yes, it is."

"And who is the commander of the resistance?"

"I don't know. I took orders from a person I only know as Hans."

"Hans? Do you know how many Hanses are in Berlin?"

"You can try to find that one," I said, grinning.

He stopped for a while, still rubbing his chin. His face lost the contours of the present. The false seed had been planted, and now I was waiting for the harvest.

"I think you're lying," he said in a low voice.

I said nothing, relaxing my muscles and forcing my mouth corners to keep a grin on my face. Adlerstein stood and began to pace the coupe from the window to the door and back. I decided to go on with this false story, moving his mind as far from the truth as possible.

"No," he said, "You're not from the resistance. Well, not from the resistance that operated in Berlin."

He stopped pacing and bent closer to my face. "The Berlin resistance was completely destroyed. I wonder why you didn't hear about it. It was in the newspaper."

Adlerstein straightened and crossed his arms over his chest.

"But I know that firsthand." He paced a few more steps. "I know that because it was I who destroyed it."

His steps ceased. "You are a British agent who stopped the train and was ordered to free our prisoner." He nodded. "You should have read the newspapers. You would have known everything necessary to support your lies."

A faded memory blinked from the deepness of my brain. Yes, I did remember. It was written everywhere, even in Dutch newspapers. No one mentioned Adlerstein's name, though. This moron was lying. What was he up to serving me his lies? Or did he just want to look like a hero in front of me? Impress me?

"You're lying," I said in a calm voice. "Your name wasn't mentioned in the newspapers."

His face twitched, and his cheeks reddened. Sudden rage hardened the shape of his face, tensing his facial muscles inward. Adlerstein stiffened for several moments and then took a deep breath. He succeeded in controlling it.

I continued. "You're shooting blind. You have no tiny idea what's going on here. You don't know who I am. You just guessed when you met me. It was a coincidence." My pretend smile changed to a real one. In my mind, I felt a huge stone falling off my heart. The tension in my muscles disappeared. I was tied, and on my way to die, but the information about Amsterdam's resistance was still secure.

He leaned closer to my face. I smelled his breath stinking of stomach acid. This bloke was nervous like a lone swimmer in a pool full of sharks.

"I don't care what you think," he whispered through his clenched teeth. "I don't care whether you're lying or not. I will bring you to the people who specialize in getting the truth from crooks like you."

He exhaled and took another deep breath.

"There's only one thing I can promise to you. You are going to suffer. Suffer like never before. Every minute of your life will feel like an hour. In the end, you will beg for death. You will beg for mercy because the only redemption for you will be a bullet to your head. But I promise you that that will never happen, and you will die in brutal pain."

He swung his arm and slapped my face. My head tilted, but it didn't hurt. I only felt the warmth of the blood rushing into my cheeks. Adlerstein knew nothing. He didn't know about Anna and Simon. He was genuinely convinced that I was a British spy. I liked it.

Adlerstein spun and opened the coupe door, swaying it with such a force that the door bounced off the wall and returned, almost closing itself again. The soldier holding his MP40 in an attack position peered inside.

"Guard this prisoner! I will demand your head if he escapes!"

The soldier nodded.

"And put him on the floor. His legs in front, so he will face the window!" He stepped out of the coupe.

The hands grabbed me and put me down.

Chapter 24

I lay on the cold floor in the coupe between two seats. The door wasn't completely closed, leaving a narrow gap. The draft flowing from there cooled my sore head. How many times had I said to myself today that this was over? That all my efforts had been pointless, and there was no way out? But this crazy story kept going. My hands had been tied behind my back, and my legs were tied together. Four belts were fastened over my body, each one extremely tight. One crushed my chest, squeezing my lungs, another squeezed my waist. Two more clamped down on my legs, causing pins and needles. Impossible to get out of this. I would be delivered like a parcel straight to the hands of the worst investigator within the SS, *Obersturmführer* Herman von Dahrt. He would be sur-prised to see me.

The blood hummed in my ears. They would execute me in the backyard, that was for sure. An alleged Dutch spy executed for the glory of the Third Reich. At least I hadn't revealed Anna's and Simon's identities. Not so far. I rather didn't think how they could get this information during the torture. Needed to escape before the train reached Berlin. Or die. An image of that poor Frenchman flashed through my mind. Perhaps I could provoke them to kill me. Yes, I'd rather die of a bullet while running away than betray friends under torture. I opened my eyes.

I faced the window. Gloom crept into the car. Outside, the sun was saying good night. The sky wore a gleaming golden coat. I rolled my eyes up and, tilting my head back, spotted the silhouette of a soldier standing before the door facing the corridor. Another silhouette approached. They gesticulated and whispered something I couldn't understand, and then the soldier's silhouette left. Changing the guards.

The second silhouette moved and opened the door. I returned my sight to the window. He stamped on the floor. Heavy army boots. I closed my eyes. I didn't want to see him. Not now.

"Shhh," the voice whispered. "Don't move."

"I'd like to move, but I can't. Maybe you didn't notice, but I'm trussed up like a Christmas present," I whispered back.

"Shhh."

Two hands twisted me around, and a rhythmical move wobbled my hands. The occasional touch of cold steel. The man was cutting my ties. I opened my eyes and lifted my face from the floor. All I could see was a gray-green uniform. An ugly uniform.

"What are you doing?" I whispered.

"What do you think? Cutting those fucking ties," the voice said, speaking up a bit.

Stefan! What the hell is he doing?

"Stefan, let it be. They will execute you when they find out you released me."

"Fuck 'em all. I don't care."

I grinned. The change in his speech was amusing. "What a change in your vocabulary. I thought you were a teacher."

"Yes. I am a teacher and want to teach what's right and true, not what I was told to teach."

He finished cutting the rope binding my hands, pulled me up, and sat me on the seat.

"Finish it. I will guard." His arm stretched, handing me the knife.

"I can't move my hands until you undo these belts on my chest and waist."

"Shit!"

He pulled at the belt to release the buckle, but it hurt me, tugging the skin on my chest. The buckle didn't even move.

"Ouch! Don't do that, please. You must cut it."

Stefan stuck the knife's blade under the belt and sawed. The knife was dull, like a piece of wood. Each stroke made me want to cry out in pain. I tried to hold my breath as much as possible.

"Hurry!" I said, clenching my teeth.

"I'm getting tired. Who bought these knives for the army? Another useless business for the state treasury."

He sawed at the belt, opening and closing his mouth with each stroke. I tensed my arm, pushing against the belt. After a while, it cracked. My lungs whistled as I took a huge breath in.

"Shit, I'm tired," he said.

"Would you, please, stop cursing? Focus on the second belt."

He tilted his head down and began the second operation. His hand moved slower and slower. After a while, the second belt cracked and fell to the floor.

The rest went easier. I unfastened the belts on my legs and stood up. The blood began to flow again, causing a sudden wave of heat. The feeling of sharp needles pricking through my muscles slowly faded. The hasty re-lief trembled my muscles. I stood and jumped several times to help the blood to fill up quicker.

"What now? "Stefan said, casting his sad eyes at me.

"We have to leave before someone comes. Let's hide in a different coupe. There you can explain what the hell you were doing. And I'm really curious what you'll say."

He turned and tensed, ready to run, but I stopped him.

"No, not there."

"What?"

"We can't run into the hands of other soldiers."

"But we are in the first car. Where else would you run?"

I pointed my finger. "To the first coupe."

"What?"

"Where will they look when they find out I disappeared?"

He chuckled, nodding his head. "A good one."

I closed the door and locked it. The heavy red curtains on the sides of the door covered us. We sat on the floor between seats, Stefan aiming his MP40 at the door.

My wound began to bleed again. I put my jacket down and, using Stefan's dull knife, ripped a piece of cloth off the bottom of my shirt's left front. Two more, and I would have no shirt at all.

"So, tell me what seized your brain and told you to do what you did?" I said, wrapping the cloth over my arm.

"Are you mad at me for releasing you?"

"No, of course not. I'm sorry. I should have thanked you first. So, thank you, Stefan. And I mean it."

"You're welcome." He grinned.

"But tell me why?"

He sighed. "I... I decided I no longer wanted to contribute to all this. To The Third Reich. I've never liked it. Why should I do what I hate to do?"

I understood how hard it was for him. Everything. To accept how things were. To take how things should be and were not. And to accept that he could do something about it.

"You're absolutely right. But you must hide from now on. Are you aware that you broke your vow? They will hunt you till your death," I said.

"Yes, I'm a traitor."

"How do you feel about that?"

"You know what? I've never felt better." He chuckled, but then his face went sad. Just like I'd seen it before. "You said you can get me out of the country. To Latin America. Right?"

"Not me personally. But, yes, I can help you. I know people. Help me, please." I nodded at my wounded arm.

He leaned over and began to tie a knot. "Are they willing to help me? I'm a German."

"They don't judge people by where they were born. It's what you do that matters. Ouch! Too much. Release it a bit, please."

"Then there's no problem." He finished the knot and leaned back.

"All right. We'll find a good spot and jump off the train."

"What? Wait! I thought we were going to free the prisoner."

"There's no point to it. We must save our lives. I'll go to Latin America with you."

"How? No. Wait!"

His face reddened. He stood and paced the coupe, leaping over my knees. After a while, he sat next to me, leaning against the seat.

"I'm wondering, what happened to all that freedom and other bullshit you were talking about?"

"I'm not getting it, Stefan."

"You said that. Your words. If the SS gets the information from the spy, there will be no freedom in the world. And now you don't want to free him?"

"I'd love to, but we can't do it."

"Of course, we can!"

"No, we can't." I shook my head. "Look, how would you approach the car where they're keeping him? With one gun? We'd better jump off the train as soon as we can."

"I don't want to leave without trying. We can make something up. Find some solution. There's a solution to each problem."

I shrugged. "What could we possibly do? Curse them? Do you know some voodoo spells?"

"I don't know what to do. You're a detective or soldier, or whatever you are. I'm a teacher. And I don't believe in voodoo."

"See, that's the first problem."

"What? That I don't believe in voodoo?"

"No, that you're a teacher. You have zero combat experience."

He put his hands on his waist and cocked his head. "That wasn't a problem when you asked me for help."

"That was a different situation."

"How different?"

"I had support from the outside and way more time."

"Support?"

I told him everything about the message and the attack, keeping names out. How they had tried and lost their lives. I skipped the part with the fake British spy Adlerstein. I didn't want to look like an idiot.

"You should do it for them," he said.

"Come on! This is not a school play when you can motivate children by provoking them into action."

"I mean, for their memory."

"No."

His face got even sadder. "No?"

I shook my head.

"Why?" he said in a low voice.

I sighed. "I can't do it alone."

"I'm here. Doesn't matter that I have no experience."

"No."

"Oh, for God's sake, why?"

"Because I don't trust you, Stefan! That's why!"

He lowered his head and dropped his shoulders, collapsing on the seat. His eyes gaze to nowhere.

"Come on, Stefan. Nothing personal. Just a bad experience of the last couple of hours," I said.

"Adlerstein, right? He fooled you."

I tensed up. "How do you know that?"

215

"He yelled it out so loudly that it could be heard on the moon. Every detail of how he pretended to be a Scotsman…"

I swallowed and felt the warmth of my blood reddening my cheeks. What a stupid feeling!

"Don't feel sorry for that. No one would've known that," Stefan said.

Easy to say. Hard to cope with it.

Stefan slapped his thigh. "Fuck Adlerstein! Let's focus on how to free the prisoner. We can do it!"

I shook my head. "And not to mention that there's no time."

"How come?"

"Two hours, maybe less, to Berlin. We are already too close."

"Who told you that?"

"Told me what?"

"That there are only two hours to Berlin."

"Adlerstein."

"He fooled you. We have at least four hours. I believe we have more than four hours. The train has stopped more often and waited way longer than planned. We haven't passed Hanover yet. Adlerstein even gave an order not to stop at any station until the train arrived in Berlin. He's chasing the lost time."

Chapter 25

"Are you kidding?" I said.

"I'm dead serious."

I gazed at him. A part of his enthusiasm grabbed me, I had to admit that. He was fully armed. The MP40, four full mags, and two hand grenades. Perhaps we could do something with them. Passing the outer guards, shooting them, or something. What then? Four others were waiting inside the car. Only one man could pass the door. Me or him. Two men would die, but the rest would kill me. Or him. We could use the grenades, tossing them inside the car. But, the risk of harming the prisoner was too high. I didn't believe the blankets that covered him would protect him. A dead man wouldn't reveal any secrets to the Nazis, though. I kept it as the last option.

"Erik! Erik!" Stefan said, shaking my shoulder. "Wake up! Erik!"

I lifted my head. "What?! I was thinking."

"Shhh," he said, putting his finger on his lips.

We listened. Someone shouted in the corridor. Then, someone else. A door slammed. The steps rumbled, fading into the distance.

"So, what's the plan?" he said, when the noise disappeared.

"There's no plan because you interrupted me."

"No, I really want to know what's the plan. I think we can shoot them all."

"No, we can't."

"Why?"

I explained my thoughts. He grinned when I finished.

"Another false information you've got. Adlerstein again, right?"

"What's your point?"

"The guards in the prison car, you know?"

"What with them?"

"They haven't been doubled. There are two men only."

"Two men?"

"Yes, two men. If we shoot the four men at the door, we can shoot those two as well, right?"

"Theoretically, yes. Don't forget that the noise from shooting will lure the rearguards. The windows on gangway doors are not blind. They will not only hear the shooting but also see us shooting. And there's the sig-nalization."

"See us, hear us, a signalization. You're more confusing than the Stomachion puzzle."

"What's that?"

"The oldest known mathematical puzzle that dates to the era of Archimedes." He sighed. "What now?"

"Let's focus on what options we have." I pointed at him. "Starting with the grenades. How could we use them?"

"Unscrew the cap, yank the cord out, throw it toward the target…"

"I know that. I mean, in what way we could use them?"

He pulled one grenade out and spun it in his hands. "To kill the vanguards?"

"The noise. You're always forgetting the noise."

"Erik, if we solely focus on the noise, we will never find the solution."

"It's important to eliminate the risk as much as possible. So, let's repeat it. Four men as vanguards. Four men as the rearguards. And two men in the prison car. Plus, resting off-duty soldiers in the car behind. And two grenades."

He sighed again. His face went back to his normal state of sadness, losing the light in his eyes. I felt sorry for him, but his eagerness was dangerous and could lead to his death. Many had died because they hadn't thought of all the possibilities. I didn't want to be one of them.

"Stefan, I'm sorry," I said. "Look, the battlefield is not the excellent one, but not a desperate one. There are two of us, right? How many are of them, huh? Whatever we plan, we need an advantage."

"What do you mean? What kind of advantage?"

"Like, luring the guards away from the door. Then we could pretend to be them, allowing us to enter the car with the spy without raising suspicion."

He nodded and began to scratch his temple.

"We can use it," he said.

"Use what? Grenades?"

"No, what you've just said. We can pretend you are a prisoner and me an escort. We can then pass the outer guards," he said.

"Yes, but the guards will still be there. Imagine four MP40s behind us, two in front of us…"

He waved his hand to stop me. "Got it!"

His fingers scratched his temple again. Then, it struck me out of nowhere.

"Stefan, we are permanently forgetting one important fact!"

"What fact?"

"The main guards have the alarm button!"

He snapped his fingers. "Shit, you're right. They can call the other soldiers for help. What the hell I was thinking when I said it would be easy?"

"You didn't say it would be easy."

"Good. What now?"

"To figure out how to get rid of all soldiers."

He closed his eyes and leaned his head back, keeping his mouth open. "Wait until the exchange," he said after a while.

"Worse. Eighteen soldiers will be there."

"Yes, that's true." He hung his shoulders. "No! Wait! Twenty."

"Twenty what?"

"Twenty soldiers will be there. Eight plus eight plus four."

I nodded. I would have never argued with a teacher about math. We both sank into our thoughts again.

"What about decoupling the train?" he said, slapping his thigh.

"Go on!"

"We, somehow, decouple the train right between the prison car and the car with the rear guards. That will get rid of the soldiers. With most of the soldiers gone, the train is more or less empty. And, if we are lucky..."

I raised my hand to shush him. I needed to think this through undisturbed. He was on the right track, no doubt. Decoupling the train would put half of the train out of the game. The half with most of the soldiers. Yes, if we were lucky. How to do that? The thrust from the locomotive kept the couplers locked. No way to turn them without a long lever. I gazed at Stefan. He held the grenade by the handle, spinning it in his hands, playing with it.

"We install both grenades on the coupling right behind the prison car. The explosion will decouple the train, leaving most of the soldiers behind," I said.

Surprise made his mouth drop open, and he stopped playing with the grenade, staring at me as if I was the ghost of his ancestor who came to scare the shit out of him.

"How do you want to do it? How will you pass the cars without shooting the guards?"

"Each car has an open gangway, right? And a ladder at each end, right?"

"Ahhh, that way. Instead of going through the car, you want to go over the roof. That's clever."

"Yes, that's how I got here. But we must be quiet when on the roof. However, the rumbling of the train will drown out most of our steps. Installing the grenades and setting them off, and then we will face six men only. If we are lucky."

He raised his finger. "How to install the grenades?"

"We can bind them to the coupling with the rope I was tied with. Can you bring it?"

"That won't be a problem, I think." He scratched his temple. "But another thing will be. The timing will be a problem. No one can run to safety in four seconds."

"Could you find another, way longer, rope or string?"

"I can try. What for?"

"To extend the cord and set the grenade off from the car's roof."

His face brightened, shining again with the energy rush. "Sounds good to me."

"To me, too," I said.

This could work. My shirt felt glued to my back, sticky with dried sweat. A brisk image of me having a shower burst into my thoughts. Home, sweet home. When this was over, I wouldn't leave the bathtub for three days. Or better, I would visit Sauna Deco on Herengracht. They had a pool and served French sulfurous mineral water for health. It stank of sulfur like a thousand hells but did well for the stomach and nerves.

"Stefan, I've got an idea," I said.

"What is it?"

"The vanguard. Four soldiers."

"What about them?"

"I know how force them to leave the car!"

He gazed at me again, and I again felt like a ghost.

"Do you remember the bottles with ammonium sulfide? In the mail car?"

He closed his eyes. "Yes. The fertilizer. What with that?"

"We will pour it into the ventilation chimney on the roof. It will create such a strong stench no one can bear. They will leave the car."

Stefan chuckled, tilting his head back. "Oh, wait! What if they leave the car and go to the prison car?"

"No worries," I explained to him how I would wait on the prison car's roof and shoot them on the gangway if they left there. He liked this idea.

"Wait here," he said and stood up.

Stefan left, slamming the door behind him. His heavy boots rumbled away. My mind went to a dark place. He was the only one who left for me on this train. Could I trust him? What if this was just another trap set by Adlerstein? That was possible. However, I couldn't find any reason for it. Why would Adlerstein let me out of captivity and have Stefan help me to free the spy? What would he gain? I took Stefan's dull knife, he hadn't taken back and hid it under my jacket. Just to be sure.

A group of soldiers passed by, making noise with their boots and guns and yelling at each other. I almost had a heart attack. They stopped right outside the coupe and discussed something I couldn't understand. Just a mur-mur coming through the closed door. I watched them from behind the curtain, huddled under the door win-dow. They gestured furiously with their hands. For a moment, it looked like they would fistfight. I would welcome it, though.

Stefan's voice joined the debate. Every fiber of my being screamed for him not to open the coupe door. He said something and the soldiers laughed. Their steps resonated farther and farther from me. But Stefan's silhouette moved toward the mail car. The clever bloke had done everything to protect our hideout. After a while, the door opened, and Stefan slipped in.

"They are searching the train. Adlerstein found out you disappeared," he said, closing the door. "I told them I saw someone running away." He put the bottle on the floor.

"I don't care what you said to them. Did you get a string?"

"Yes, I have it. Long enough to wrap around twenty Adlersteins. The mailman gave it to me."

He pulled the balled string out of the pocket of his jacket. The string was thin but strong enough. I couldn't tear it using just my hand.

"Good. This will do. Hand me your grenades!"

"I've got something else. Something way better," he said with pride in his voice and pulled the thing from behind his jacket.

It looked like a metal bouquet. An extremely dangerous metal bouquet. Around a central grenade six more were hitched with a single wire. *Stielhandgranate* M24 *Geballte Ladung.* He was right. This would do better.

"During my training, I heard one officer say that M24 had no sufficient power," He weighted it in his hand and then looked at me. "I saw this baby rip a truck apart."

Chapter 26

The wind blew like crazy. Or, at least, I felt it that way. The old steam locomotive couldn't go at such a high speed. Not on these old, worn rails. Perhaps it blew from the side. It didn't matter now. I'd stepped down the ladder, leaving Stefan on the roof of the prison car. We had a plan. Not a perfect one, but feasible. With a huge portion of luck, though. Still better than nothing. We had left the bottle of ammonium sulfide on the roof of the vanguard's car bound to the ventilation chimney. I che-cked the mega grenade for the last time. We had already attached the string to its cord. Now I just had to attach the whole thing to couplers and pull the string. I scanned the country running by. The sun was touching the trees on the horizon. It would set in an hour and a half, two at most.

No one had seen me so far. Before climbing down the ladder, I'd spotted a soldier's head through the window on the door. He faced the inside, not paying attention to what was happening outside. The railing fenced off the gangway. I crouched, getting closer to the edge of the gangway, and lifted the metal plate placed from one end to another over the coupling. It served as a walkway when passing between cars. I flipped it to the side, but it fell onto the rails. It bounced off the wooden ties and landed in a ditch. I ignored it. No need for a thing like that after this. The noise coming from the wheels drowned out the clanging and screeching the falling plate had produced.

Couplers were in the middle between the bumpers. The couplers' knuckles locked together, tensing, and releasing as the two cars knocked into each other. I reached over the gangways' edge, but my arm was too short. The curse of small men. Holding the railing, I reached out and touched the nearest coupler. No way to bind the grenade with one hand only. I had to stretch out over the bumpers like an acrobat. *Mighty universe, help me, please!*

Getting my legs down on the rounded bumper casing was easy. The hard part was to keep them there. The train danced like a drunken sailor. A layer of grease that had developed on the surface made it slippery. The most stupid thing was that the bumper casings were mostly under the gangway. Twisting and bending, I crouched under the gangway, holding the railing with both hands. The grenade waited in my jacket, together with the string.

One wrong step and the wheels of the cars would chop me like lettuce for a salad. I leaned back a bit, but my foot slipped, and I landed on my crotch. Nothing painful happened. A new problem occurred, though. Now, I faced the car, not the couplers. I began cursing myself for this stupid idea and letting the plate fall off. I could've used it as a bench, putting it over the bumpers.

The second attempt to ride the train like a horse went in a more relaxed way. I knew what to expect when balancing on top of the rounded surface. I was sitting on the bumper casing and squeezed it with my thighs. It shook as if it was a wild mustang. A clear picture through the eyes of rodeo riders. I tried to create a fulcrum on the spot where the coupler mounted to the car, but it was too high. My knee brushed against my chin, and that created a tension that was pushing me off the bumper because I couldn't bend over. Putting my leg into the loop of the air brake hose hanging below the coupler stabilized my position a bit. Just a bit.

The country flew past me, blurring as I gazed through the narrow space between two cars. The air stream got colder. It blew up from beneath the cars, inflating my jacket. Time to move. I reached toward the coupler with both hands. The bumpers crashed into each other, the car shook, and, pushing my leg down, I disassembled the joint on the air brake hose. Half of the train lost braking power. Never mind. Sitting on the bumper became unbearable, though. I had to hold the edge of the gangway with one hand. Changing my tactics was inevitable.

I got up, helped again by the railing, and stepped on the coupler's body. A last gaze, a last goodbye to the world, and I leap forward, putting one foot on the second coupler's body. I stood there like a statue of Helios, the wonder of Rhode Island, spreading my legs over the imaginary port. The dance didn't stop, but it was more bearable. Twisting my feet, I lowered my bottom and bent over the couplings. Stefan lay on the roof, biting his nails. I gave him a thumbs-up and almost fell, losing my balance for a moment.

In my pocket waited three pieces of string, already cut to the proper length. I pulled the grenade out of my jacket and laid it on the coupler joint, its cord facing forward. Holding it with one hand, I took one string out and flipped it over the handle. I reached underneath the couplers. The train staggered, but I kept my position. My fingers touched the second end of the string. I stretched more. The train rocked in an enormous swing, and I lost contact with the back coupler, waving my hands to restore my balance. An image of a dead body cut in halves by the train wheel flashed through my mind. My body, to be more precise.

Thanks to some invisible magic, I stood up again with my legs on each coupler. Stefan waved at me like a welcomer in the madhouse, pointing his other hand down. A glimpse at both sides. I awaited a bullet. No soldiers. Nobody. What was he up to? I shook my head and looked down. To my surprise, the only thing I held was one string. I couldn't see the other end. It went somewhere beneath the coupling. I lowered and waited until my eyes got used to the shadows.

I spotted the grenade. It danced in the air stream below the couplings, swirling around hanging by its cord. Carefully, I lifted it, praying all the time. This went past the limits of my patience. I had to speed up. My wounded arm began to hurt.

I sat on the back coupler's body and let my legs stick beneath it, risking a fall. It was narrow, digging between my buttocks, but it didn't bother me. I tied a knot over the grenade's handle in the middle of the string piece. Pressing the grenade with one hand against the coupler, I wrapped the string around it. Tying the first knot went fine. I figured out I could hold the grenade in place by pressing my forehead against it. The second piece of the string was child's play.

I lifted my head and saw a face staring at me through the window. I froze. Our eyes locked. *Shit! What now?*

The face was blurred because of the dirty glass. Had that person spotted me? Why didn't he shoot? Why didn't he yell? I thought that he nodded at me, greeting me like a good friend. Did he think I was a soldier doing something there? I looked down. The gray-green color of my uniform didn't blend with my environment. He must have seen me.

I peeked at the window again. The face was gone. I rubbed my eyes. Yes, he was gone. Were my nerves playing a strange game with my consciousness? Cursing in my mind and holding the launcher string in my teeth,

I climbed back to the roof and lay next to Stefan. He welcomed me with the gaze of a pissed-off man.

"Why the hell did you throw that plate away?! You could have laid on it!" He had to shout. The noise from the flowing air deafened our ears.

"Is the grenade in its place or not?!"

"I almost died of worry!"

"I almost died of my clumsiness. Let's focus on the task! When it goes off, we must expect the guards to appear on the gangway! You must shoot them!" I said, waving the string.

Stefan racked the slide on his MP40 and disengaged the safety.

"Are you sure you can do it?!"

He mumbled something I couldn't hear because of the noise of the flowing air.

"What?!"

"I have no problem with that!"

"Have you ever killed someone?!"

He said nothing.

I handed him the string. "Hold this!"

"Why?!"

"I will fire the gun, all right?!"

Stefan sighed but unslung and gave me the submachine gun. We lay on the roof, lifting our heads and gazing at the grenade.

"Ready?!"

"Yes!"

"After four seconds, we must put our heads down, all right?!"

He gave me a thumbs-up.

"Pull the string!" I said.

He tightened the string and yanked it.

Chapter 27

The grenade detonated with a sharp crack, leaving a smoke cloud rising toward the sky. I was deaf, and for a while, the only sound I could hear was an unpleasant ringing. I lifted my upper body, supporting it on my elbows. Half of the train slowed as it lost the pull of the locomotive. A soldier's face appeared in the gangway door window. He looked surprised. Who wouldn't have been? I twitched, following the spontaneous impulse to fire at him, but he didn't pull the trigger. There was no reason to do it. Better to save some bullets. Swallowing a few times, I released the ringing.

Stefan lay on the roof, his head down, his hands pressed to his ears. I poked him with my finger. Nothing. No reaction at all. I had to grab his shoulder and jerk him. He lifted his head and turned to me, his hand still covering his ears. I nodded toward the slowing cars. He slowly released his ears and sat up.

"We did it!" he said, turning his face at me and grinning. "We got rid of them!"

I would've liked to share in his happiness, but we had to proceed with our plan. The British spy was still there, under the roof, guarded by SS soldiers.

"Let's pour the ammonium into the chimney vent!"

Stefan nodded and spun on all fours. Wobbling against the train's shocks, he began to move toward the other end of the car. I pulled the sling to park the gun on my back and followed him. It didn't go as easily as when we had been getting here. We had to fight with the airstream blowing against us. We moved, though. Slowly but forward.

At the end of the roof, Stefan jerked back, and I heard the muted sound of shooting. Then it struck me. The signalization. That fucking signalization had gone off when the cars separated. It had torn the wires. How could I have been so stupid? I gazed at Stefan, and he understood.

He moved a bit aside, making space for me. Holding the chimney vent, I pulled myself up to see what was happening down on the gangway. A batch of bullets flew in the air, fortunately, far away from my head, but before I could see who was there.

Stefan put his hands to his mouth. "*Nicht schießen*! Don't shoot!"

"What?!"

"Don't shoot, for God's sake! It's me, Stefan!"

"Stefan?!"

"I'm coming down! I have no gun!"

"All right!"

I grabbed his hand, silently asking what the hell he was about to do, but he shook his head and gazed straight into my eyes. What I saw made me release my grip. Strong determination. A will that didn't accept resistance. Pure energy flowed from him as if he were a human power plant. He nodded toward the men on the gangway and ran his finger over his throat. All my doubts about him disappeared.

Stefan rose, checking the gangway, and stood up. Helping with his hands, he turned and put his feet on the ladder. His lips whispered, "*Kill them.*" I nodded, and he disappeared.

I moved forward, praying Stefan had caught their attention, and peered down. Four men stood on the gangway, holding MP40s. One was gesturing something I couldn't understand. They were talking, but I could only hear a murmur of their voices. Then, two soldiers crossed the gangway, closing in on Stefan. I imagined he stood under the ladder, but I could see only half of the gangway. Time to take a risk.

I pulled the submachine gun off my back and aimed, holding my breath. My index finger yanked, and the MP40 barked, piercing the two men. They fell off the train.

I heard a muted *Scheize!* and the murmur amplified. The guns fired from beneath me, and a few bullets chipped the edge of the roof. I aimed at the place where the end of the ladder was fixed into the car. Anytime a barrel might show there I sent a bunch of bullets. The murmur continued.

The door underneath me slammed. More than hearing it, I felt it through my body lying on the roof. Someone yelled something. Then another voice cut through. I tried to prick my ears, but it was futile. Two soldiers appeared, jumping onto the gangway. I pulled the trigger once again. Their bodies twisted and shook when the bullets drilled holes in them. Four men down.

More yelling. Then nothing. And again yelling. And then, continuous shooting lasting at least five seconds. My blood pressure rose. Those bastards killed Stefan! There was no time for whining, though. Stefan was dead, and nothing stopped me from leaning the gun over the roof and sending a batch of bullets down. Then, I would jump and end the saddest story of my short life. Pushing with my toes, I move closer to the roof's edge. But something stopped me.

The roof vibrated. I felt it through my stomach. It wasn't the train shaking. Turning my head to the side, I spotted a hole in the roof three inches from my shoulder. I spun, getting on my back. A soldier strolled toward me, wrestling with the air stream. He wobbled right when his MP40 flashed, his hands unable to aim the gun. The flo-wing air around my ears drowned out the sound. One bullet drilled an ugly hole into the metal plate on the ventilation chimney.

My submachine gun sent a batch of bullets at him. The car was rocking from side to side. A splash of blood. The soldier halted and put his hand on his right side. Blood flowed from behind his palm. One bullet had torn his trousers and scratched his bare skin. I pulled the trigger again, but nothing happened. He limped again, holding the submachine gun with one hand only.

A glance at the open chamber assured me the mag was empty. Instinctively, I reached around to my back, but there was nothing. *Shit!* Stefan had the mags! He'd handed me the gun, but all the magazines had remained in his pouch.

The soldier stopped before my legs, aiming the MP40 at me.

"Who are you?!" he said in German.

I said nothing. My whole body tensed in one big spasm. These were the last seconds of my life. I didn't want to spend them talking to a Nazi fucker.

"Who are you?!"

I gazed straight into his eyes.

His finger pulled the trigger. The back blow lifted the gun's barrel, and the bullet went to the space between the sky and the earth. He wasn't strong enough to shoot with one hand only.

He moved closer, standing between my legs, wobbling with the rhythm of the car's shocks. He bent his knees to stabilize his posture.

"Who are you?"

I sprang my leg and kicked him hard in his wounded side. He shouted in pain, pressing both hands to his side and leaving his MP40 hanging loosely on his shoulder.

With all my strength, I sat up and grabbed the gun's sling. Twisting my upper body, I sprang my leg and kicked him again into his wounded leg. He jerked back, but my hands pulled stronger. He bent and let the sling slip off his shoulder. I didn't expect it and fell back. The gun slammed to the roof, sending bullets to the country running around us, and fell off the roof.

The soldier reached for his belt. A pistol. I knew it very well. Walther P38. Another gun rattled behind me, and the soldier's body jerked in a crazy dance and then fell off the roof.

I turned.

Stefan's face was pale. He stood on the ladder, half of his body over the roof. His gun was still ready to shoot. He winked, and his head disappeared.

I sat and took a deep breath, relaxing a bit and letting the wind cool me down. This was draining my energy. There were supposed to be six soldiers only. Where the hell had the last one come from? Could we expect more of them in the prison car?

I got on all fours and approached the ladder. Stefan was waiting below. My leg trembled when I stepped on the ladder rung. Stefan helped me, and we stood next to each other. Two dead bodies lay on the gangway.

"What now?" he said, leaning close to my ear.

"Thank you, Stefan."

"Don't mention it. We are even. You saved my life when the plane was firing at us. What now?"

"I thought you were dead."

"Why?"

"They shot."

"I shot. What now?"

"Let's check what's happening inside."

I peered through the corner of the door window. Inside, it was dark, but I spotted three gray uniforms.

"There are soldiers inside."

"What now?" Stefan said again.

"Jump off the train?"

He shook his head. And he was right. His energy struck me, and I forgot everything I had been thinking of a minute ago.

"Hm, we no longer need to pour ammonium sulfide into the chimney. Now, we can play the soldier and the captive and step into the car," I said.

"How will we do that?"

"I will hide the MP40 behind my back and put my hands there, too, as if they are tied. When in, we get closer and shoot them."

"Sounds good to me."

"Don't forget to talk a lot. That will distract them."

He nodded.

"Ready?"

He nodded.

I stepped around him, approaching the door from the side. Taking full mags from the dead soldiers who wouldn't need them anymore, I put them into the pouch on my back and loaded the gun. Stefan adjusted the sling on his gun so it hung below his chest and reached for the door handle, waiting for me. I hid my MP40 behind my back and nodded.

Stefan opened the door before me. Three soldiers aimed their guns right at my head.

Chapter 28

"We got him!" Stefan said, sticking his head to the door. "He will wait here with the prisoner. *Hauptsturmführer* Adlerstein's orders. No one can touch him or harm him."

The soldiers stood in the space between two seat sections. They were still aiming at me. The weak electric lamps installed along the car lit the space with dirty yellow light.

"Give up, Stefan!" one soldier said. "We saw you climbing down the ladder!"

I knew his face. One of the soldiers from my squad.

"Yes. I got him on the roof."

"So, what was that shooting for?"

"He was defending himself like a madman. He got the others, but not me. I got him."

"Don't lie, Stefan!"

"You dare to call me a liar?!" Stefan's body got taller. He pushed me forward and followed. We strolled towards aiming guns. The car looked the same as I had seen it before. A few seats were missing, as well as the disassembled vestibule in the middle that would typically separate the car sections. The prisoner was in another section. I spotted his legs sticking out from the seat he was lying on.

"Give up, Stefan!"

Stefan put his hand on my shoulder and sat me on the nearest seat closer to the aisle.

"Look, I don't care," he said and sat on the seat across the aisle. "I can wait till Adlerstein comes. He will explain everything."

When the back of the seat before me concealed my hands, I pulled the submachine gun from behind my back, keeping it invisible to soldiers' eyes.

The soldiers relaxed and began to whisper, talking to each other, but their hands ready to pull the triggers.

"Put your gun down, Stefan!" one of them said after a while.

"Forget it!"

"We are the guardians of the prison car, not you. You don't need a gun."

"If I put my gun down, this bloke here will run away," Stefan said and drew a cigarette out of the pocket. I didn't know he was a smoker. The lighter flicked, and blue-grayish smoke floated around his head.

"All right. Bring him here."

"No," Stefan said. "If you want him, come over and take him. You called me a liar, *kamerad*. I'd rather wait for Adlerstein."

"I will escort him here," one soldier said and paced toward us.

We looked at each other, sending signals. Stefan flicked his eyes toward the soldier. I shook my head slightly. We had to wait until the soldier got closer. Stefan nodded.

The soldier approached my seat. I grabbed the barrel of his submachine gun and pulled it. He bent forward. With my other hand, I pressed my MP40 to his chest and pulled the trigger. His heavy body falling on me. I jumped closer to the window and let it drop to the floor.

Meanwhile, Stefan fired at the rest of them. One soldier fell dead. The last one jumped aside, his submachine gun shooting everywhere except at us. He hid behind the seat where lay the prisoner, sticking out the gun's barrel.

"Anton, give up!" Stefan said, changing his mag. "You don't need to die!"

"You betrayed us, Stefan! Just yesterday we sang together *Teufelslied.* And today? Look at you!"

Stefan racked the slide and glanced at me. I shook my head. Impossible to shoot. The risk of injuring the prisoner was too high.

"Yes, I did betray the *Waffen-SS,* but because I was betrayed in the first place."

"That's bullshit! No one betrayed you. But you will pay!"

His gun began to bark. Completely unnecessarily. He didn't look at where he was aiming, and all the bullets hit the ceiling. Thankfully, the gun's roaring didn't last a long time.

"Anton," Stefan said, "I could kill you here and now. That seatback is like paper. But I won't. Just to show you I'm dead serious. You can walk out."

The soldier said nothing.

"You don't need to die, Anton!"

The soldier kept silent. Something clicked like two metals bumping into each other. That bloke was changing mags. Opportunity.

I tossed the gun away and leaped to the aisle, accelerating toward him. That made enough noise for him to notice. Glancing at me, he sprang into the aisle, pulling the gun's slide back. I stretched my hands out and jumped, hitting him hard in the chest. He fell back, using his hands as bumpers. I landed on him. The slide clacked loudly. I had a feeling that was the last sound I would hear before I died. In a millisecond, I was on my knees, grasping the submachine gun. He pushed like crazy, trying to twist the gun out of my hands and pointing it at me. I jerked my hand up and straightened my legs. The gun's sling slipped off him, but my foot tripped, and I fell backward. The gun flew away.

With the speed of a cat, he sprung and reached out, trying to nail me to the floor. I pulled his hands and thrust my legs, lifting his hips, and threw him over my head. His body rumbled when he hit the floor. I stood up and turned. The submachine gun lay on the floor in the middle of the empty space. We both rocketed toward it.

The soldier jumped forward and grabbed the gun. I crashed into him, and when he fell, the gun's sling slipped over his head. With all my strength, I pulled the sling with both hands and stuck my knee deep in between his shoulder blades. The gun's body was crushing his throat. I pulled more, lifting his head off the floor. He grunted but pressed with both hands against the gun's body.

It lasted forever. My arms weakened, and the sweat poured over my body. How much time was necessary to strangle a man?

The soldier stopped pushing and twisted. I fell aside. His head released from behind the gun's body, and the gun hit my chest. I grabbed it and pointed at him.

He was already on his knees, halfway to standing up. Our eyes locked. His impassive face hardened.

"A big hero, huh?! Kill me!"

I did.

His body fell back, landing on the other soldier's dead body. I knew his face. This bloke had stared at me when I'd been installing the grenade. Why hadn't he raised the alarm right there? No way he could not have seen me when I had been installing the grenade.

Stefan approached and helped me to stand up. The huge relief reflected on his face.

"We did it, Erik!" he said. "We fucking did it!" He raised his hands, waving them up and down, celebrating prematurely.

"It's not over yet," I said and tossed the gun next to the dead bodies. "Let's check the spy. I hope he didn't catch a bullet. And hurry up. Someone could enter anytime. This half of the train was supposed to have guards only, for God's sake."

We moved toward the seat. The British spy lay there, tied like a parcel. He had a gag in his mouth.

"Sir Edmund Thorne, don't worry. We're here to save you," I said, keeping my voice as calm as possible.

With help from Stefan, we sat the poor bloke up. I began to undo the gag. It was kept in place by a piece of clothes knotted behind his head. Stefan undid the knot on the rope wrapped around the spy's body. It went easily. I handed him his knife, and he began to cut the rope that tied the spy's hands, huffing like a rhino.

"Don't let these uniforms mislead you. I'm Dutch, Erik Jansen. This is Stefan Fischer. He helped me."

The knot on the clothes gave up. The spy spat the gag out.

"Thank you, my dear boy!" he said.

He was at least fifty years old. His messy hair and thick mustache were gray. His face wrinkled with age. The bloke wore brown tweed trousers and a yellow shirt hidden under a dark green sweater. He must have been broiling all this time. Beads of sweat dotted his forehead, and he licked his parched lips.

Stefan finished, and the rope fell to the floor. He handed him his water canteen. The spy put the flask on his lips and gulped the water.

"Drink slowly, sir. We don't want you to faint or get sick," I said.

"I must say, your face is familiar to me," Sir Edmund Thorne said. "If memory serves, you were casting quite the intent gaze in my direction as you passed this very carriage."

"Yes, it was me. I was checking on you. Anna Bakker sent me to free you."

"Anna Bakker?"

"Do you know her?"

"No."

"Then…"

He stopped me with a gesture. "I dare say that particular nomenclature had graced my ears sometime prior. If I'm not mistaken, it was a matter of months before my journey to the Netherlands commenced."

"Why did you come?"

"That's classified, my dear boy. I'm afraid I must exercise the utmost discretion on that particular matter."

"I understand."

Stefan straightened and tossed the cut rope onto the floor. "Done."

The spy lifted his hands and waved them until the blood started flowing in his veins.

"What shall we do now?" he said.

"Now, we need to jump off the train. Can you do it?"

"One should be equal to the challenge, I expect."

"But be aware that we could end up dead."

"I daresay any alternative would be preferable to enduring the rather unpleasant ministrations of those Gestapo chaps in their Berlin basement," he said and stood up from the seat, radiating determination.

"We should go before someone enters," Stefan said and moved toward the car's side door.

He opened it. The draft blew inside, lifting the dust and whirlpooling it. Fresh air brought a new wave of energy. Our faces brightened. The country was flat. Fields, meadows, and the road running along the railroad. The sun's last beams lit the sky, coloring the clouds orange. The railroad was separated from the road by a wide ditch with grass growing on it. Ideal for jumping.

"Don't forget to roll," I told Sir Edmund Thorne.

"Roll?"

"Yes."

"What for?"

"That should help you to survive the jump."

"See you soon, my dear friends!" he said and jumped out.

I watched him roll down the ditch slope.

"Now you!" I said to Stefan. "Quickly, I don't want to walk for a long time looking for you outside."

Stefan shook my hand and turned his head toward the gangway door. I spotted movement in the corner of my eyes. Someone was there. I twisted, and my jaw dropped.

Hauptsturmführer Adlerstein strode from the gangway door, holding a pistol and aiming it at us.

Chapter 29

Adlerstein lifted his hand and shot three times at Stefan, who, holding the vertical handle installed next to the door, spun, and fell off the train without saying a word, without casting a gaze. Just fell off.

"What the hell did you do?!" I said.

"I killed the traitor."

"He was an innocent man, you idiot!"

"He was a traitor."

I leaped toward the door, but he shot again. A bullet bounced off the screw in the floor right before my feet, making whistling noise and leaving the train through the open door.

"And now, you want to kill me?" I said.

"No. I want to arrest you, bring you to Berlin, and hand you over to the investigators. Killing you would be stupid. You are my promotion." He chuckled. "Yes, my promotion."

"I must say I have no interest to be your promotion. So, goodbye," I said and stepped closer to the door.

Another bullet buzzed in the air, burrowing into the floor.

"You are going nowhere."

"Why?"

"I've already told you. You're my promotion, Mr. British agent."

"A British agent? I'm not a British agent, for God's sake. I've already told you."

"Don't be silly. I knew about you even before you got on this train."

"I'm not a British agent, you idiot!"

"Enough lies!" His face hardened. "You stopped the train when the plane came to bomb us. That was smart. All the time, you wanted to kill my prisoner. And you did it before I could stop you."

"Stopped the train? And how did I do that? By whistling? I wanted to free the spy, you moron, not kill him."

"Then why did you throw him out of the car?"

"What?! He jumped by himself!"

I lifted my foot. He shot again.

"You are going nowhere!" he said and shot the next bullet closer to me.

I moved back. Another shot. I moved further back, keeping my muscles ready to run and jump off the train. He had to run out of bullets sooner or later. I would use the time while he changed the mag.

"I know what you are thinking of. It won't work." He grabbed the gun with his other hand and pulled out the sword he carried bound to his wide belt. The empty pistol dropped to the floor.

"What do you want to do with that ceremonial saber?" I said.

"Oh, it's not a ceremonial saber. This sword had been in our family for generations, passing from father to son. It cut off Turkish heads at Kahlenberg Mountain in the Battle of Vienna two hundred and fifty years ago."

"Bullshit. It should be rusty like devil's ass after such a long time."

"You can't insult me, British agent! I'll hand you over to the hands of justice! Third Reich justice."

"In other words, you will send me to my death."

"Yes, you might die. But after our best investigators will interrogate you."

"Those are not investigators. Who has ever heard about investigators torturing people? Your Reich lives in medieval times."

"Our Reich is the most modern in the world!"

"Your Reich is the most rotten in the world. Your government is spreading terror amongst the citizens. Because that's what corrupted pigs do."

"People love our *Führer!*"

"People fear your *Führer* and his sidekicks who sticks out of his ass."

He walked toward the door, still pointing the sword at me. If I moved there, he would leap forward and pierce my body. Adlerstein caught the door handle and yanked it. The door got stuck, but jerking, he released it and slammed it closed. My way out stopped existing.

We circled the space between two side doors in a low stance, taking sideways steps and keeping six feet apart. My senses worked one hundred and twenty percent, scanning his moves, ready to act.

"Your fate is sealed, British agent."

"It's easy for you to threaten me because you have that piece of old metal you call a saber. I have nothing. That's not fair," I said.

"It's a sword! You can't provoke me."

"Yes, unfair is the only way you understand."

He leaped forward and lunged. I sprung and twisted, but he waved his arm and slapped me with the flat surface of the sword on my buttocks. It hurt.

We circled again, my senses stimulated to the maximum.

"I can do this all day." He chuckled.

"I believe you can. You like to torture people."

"That's not true. I'm a man of honor."

"I'd love to tell you what kind of man you are, but my mother taught me not to swear in front of strangers."

"Oh, little boy. Are you calling your mama?" He swung the sword and slapped my wounded arm. I was too slow. The sharp pain flashed through my brain, paralyzing my movements. I hissed, covering the wound with my hand.

"Ts-ts-ts," he said, shaking his head.

This was a game of cat and mouse. I was the mouse. The worst position ever. We circled, eyes glued on each other's moves.

"Why didn't you arrest me sooner if you were so sure I'm the agent?" I said.

"I wanted to catch you during your action."

"Why?"

"That's a stupid question."

"That's why I'm asking you. Only you can answer stupid questions."

"Never refuse the last requests of a dying man." He chuckled again. "Arresting you during your action will skyrocket my reputation. I'll get a promotion. The position I deserve."

"You're following your needs, not the needs of Germany. You're just a status seeker."

"My needs are The Third Reich's needs."

He lunged and slapped me again, now below the wound. Then spun and slapped me on the other arm. He was fast.

I approached the dead men lying on the floor and stopped. With my eyes still locked on his eyes, I knelt, reaching for the submachine gun that lay there.

Adlerstein chuckled and lunged. My fingers touched the cold metal, but it was too late. The tip of the sword flew a few inches from my head. I lifted the gun and beat off the sword, smashing the gun's body into it. I'd got the wrong gun, though. The gun's sling hung over the neck of the dead man. The MP40 slipped out of my hands and fell back to the floor, making a dull noise. I jumped aside to safety.

"Good attempt!" Adlerstein said. "But not enough. You need to be faster."

"Fuck off!"

"Come on! No need to be rude." He grinned, knowing that he had the upper hand over me.

We circled again. I needed something I could use against his sword. He was really good at fencing. He calculated each step, each move. I couldn't overpower him with my bare hands.

I gazed around and spotted a broom leaning against the wall. The handle made of hardwood. I grabbed it.

"This should scare me?" He covered his eyes with his palm. "Ooh, I'm scared." His voice full of confidence. Perhaps he was more confident than he should be.

We circled again. I held the broom in both hands, pointing the broom's head at him. He took a sidestep, and I attacked him, sticking the bristles into his face. He twisted in a half spin and jerked forward with a stretched hand, lunging. I waved the broom, waiting for the sword's tip to stick into my chest. Adlerstein suddenly spun, cut the broom handle into two, and jumped back. The broom head fell to the floor. He kicked it away.

No one could have expected such a move. Instead of a broom, I held only a piece of its handle.

"That was good, wasn't it?" he said and bowed like a musketeer, keeping his free hand behind his back.

"You've been practicing." I waved the bare wood.

"It was part of my growing up."

"You should have practiced football instead of this."

"Phew! Football is for poor children. I'm from a noble family."

"Oh, I'm sorry. I forgot. Your shit doesn't smell. Good. I won't get poisoned when I finish with you."

"I'm getting bored," he said. "Let's make it faster." He lunged again.

I blocked the attack with the wood, parrying it aside, and twisted. He spun and faced me again, keeping his distance as before.

"Always face your adversary. That's what I was taught in the first place," he said.

"Can we just stop for a few moments and relax?"

He chuckled.

All this squatting and sideway stepping drained my energy. Sweat covered my forehead and my back once again. My throat was dry, asking for water. Adlerstein's head sweated as well. Tiny drops reflected from his forehead in this poorly lit space. I took several steps in the opposite direction. He followed. I took more steps, again changing direction. He followed. Dead bodies lay on my left, and the door was on my right. I moved closer to the door. Adlerstein stepped closer as well.

We stood still, panting and crouching. Our eyes locked. The air became heavy and moist. The lack of oxygen painted yellow-red circles in my vision. Adlerstein unbuttoned the top of his uniform and smirked. The last minutes of my life.

I flung my hand and threw the stick at him. He waved the sword but missed, and the stick hit him on the head. An oblong, bright crimson stain appeared on his forehead. I signaled to jump toward the door, stamping my boot. Adlerstein lunged, ignoring the pain, his hand holding the sword stretched.

Using the remains of my energy, I sprung and jumped to the opposite side, tumbling forward. I landed on the dead bodies, twisted, and, grabbing the submachine gun and racking the slide, I unloaded the whole magazine on him. The bullets jerked his body backward, drilling deadly holes. The window on the door behind him shattered. He fell, swimming in his own blood.

My blood pressure rose and fell almost at the very exact moment. The car began to spin, and my stomach tensed in a crazy spasm. I got on all fours and vomited.

Chapter 30

Fresh air blew across my face. It felt like a promise of new times. Times where I wouldn't need to worry about my life. But I didn't believe that feeling. I opened the side door wide, sliding both sides open. Now, leaning against them, I enjoyed the moment. The sun had already set, but the gray light of the late evening lit the countryside . Ideal for having a drink in good company. My nerves relaxed. Adlerstein was dead, and I was alive. But it wasn't over. Anytime, someone could enter the car.

I grabbed Adlerstein's dead hands and pulled his body to the door. The last gaze at him. No, no regrets. Not even a feeling of victory. I felt relief that the world was rid of one extremely conceited moron. Who knew how many good people suffered because of him? Who knew how many would have suffered in the future because of him? History would judge me, not people.

"Go to the hell, Adlerstein!" I said and kicked him out. His sword flew right behind him.

The country had changed. The train traveled on the side of the hills through a valley. White rocks beneath me reflected the weak daylight. Jumping would be like asking a Nazi soldier to send a bullet into my head. I didn't know how long a distance the train traveled while I'd been fighting. Where would I find the spy and Stefan? I recalled an image of him. The last time I'd seen him was him being shot and falling off. I prayed he was alive. Could be wounded, but alive. I just liked that bloke and the change he had gone through.

I went back and checked the dead soldiers. It wasn't a pleasant task. Blood was everywhere. Only a total creep would enjoy it. I pulled dead bodies apart. They had full mags. I tucked them everywhere I could. Behind my belt, into the inner pockets of my jacket. Putting all three MP40s in a line, I chose one. Four grenades. But my trust in them was weaker than a sheet of wet paper. I believed the train was already in Germany. A long way back stood in front of me. I wouldn't let my skin go easy off me if some other Nazis caught me. My determination to shoot my way back home was stronger than ever. One by one, I threw the dead bodies off the train. Many heads in Berlin would shake over the unbelievable disappearances.

I stood in the middle of the door, waiting for the best moment to jump. The old locomotive accelerated. Forest replaced the rocks. My head spun a bit because the trees, pines, and spruces blinked before my eyes. The smell of needles and resin filled up my nose. The smell of freedom? I liked that idea. I felt like I could touch them.

I lifted my leg, ready to jump. What if I hit the tree? I didn't care. I would die as a free man. The last deep breath.

The image of the forest disappeared, and I spotted a nice green meadow with a road running along the rail track. I grinned. I laughed, jumping, yelling, and slapping my thighs.

On the road, a car, a green Mercedes-Benz Cabriolet, ran along the railroad with the roof folded back. Simon was driving. Another man sat on the rear seat, hiding from the wind. A woman next to the driver stood up, holding the top of the windshield. Anna Bakker. Her red dress brightened the entire scenery. She, her red dress, and a lit cigarette couldn't exist without each other. I waved at them.

Anna sent signals. She pointed at me, then pointed down. I showed her a thumbs-up to confirm that I would jump off the train. She waved her hand like the tail of a fish and pointed to the distance. Message received. I didn't know why, but I understood her. There was a river or a lake, and she wanted me to jump into the water. I knew where I was. Only one railroad bridge was wide enough, and only one river was deep enough to provide a safe jump. *Elbbrücke Hämerten* over the river *Elbe*. Eighty miles to Berlin.

I waved, and the car sped up, disappearing in the distance.

How the hell had they survived the explosion? I remembered Simon sticking through the truck's roof opening and shooting at the train. It didn't make sense. He could've jumped before it had happened, though. Never mind. He would explain everything later. My eyes welled up with tears. I was happy to see him. I was happy to see them all.

We were close to the bridge. Moisture filled the air, and it began to smell of fish. Or was it just my imagination? Didn't matter. This was my way home. The brakes squealed, and the train slowed down.

The bridge deck paced underneath my legs. Timing was vital if I didn't want to end up smashed on the girders or pillars. Adrenaline rush. Three, two, one. Jump. I closed my eyes, flying through space. My hands spread.

Chapter 31

The waters of the Elbe were cold, like a piece of ice drawn straight from the fridge. The uniform soaked and glued to my skin, restricting me from swimming. But I had to. A strong current carried me to the middle of the river. I was kicking and waving my hands like it was my last day on Earth. The wound on my arm hurt, but water cooled it down a bit, so it was bearable. The bank stood in the same distance, sometimes even running away from me.

A dark boat embarked. A man, sitting on the bench, paddled with strong pulls. I unfastened the belt and let it sink with all those unnecessary things, like magazines and grenades. Way better. I'd never been a great swimmer, but I could keep my body on the water's surface. Although all my movements were ineffective and unsynchronized.

The boat approached, and the man's face took on sharper contours. He looked like Simon. Hope poured a new energy into my muscles. I sped up a bit. Twenty meters. Ten meters.

"Hold on, Erik!" Simon said.

Easier to say than to do. I stopped swimming, but the weight of the water drank by the uniform pulled me down. My legs stamped in the river, holding my face just above the level.

Simon stopped paddling and reached out. I stretched my hand as well. Simon grabbed me and pulled me, almost falling into the river. With my free hand, I grasped the boat's edge and swung my leg up, hooking it like an anchor. In a few seconds, I was sitting on the boat bench, wet and cold but happy. Simon spread a heavy army blanket around me.

"Why do I always have to pull you from the water?" Simon said, laughing.

"I don't know. I just like to bathe when you're around."

"Good to see you, Erik."

"Good to see you, too. Thank you, Simon. You saved my life once again."

"No, I didn't. You weren't drowning like the last time."

I turned, expecting to see the others. My body trembled, and my teeth chattered from the cold.

Simon read my thoughts. "You can't see them, Erik. They are behind the bank, on the road."

"I hope they made a fire. Otherwise, I will freeze to death."

"No worries. Anna will find a quick solution."

We arrived. Simon jumped out and pulled the boat to the shore. I stepped to the solid ground, and my heart pounded for a moment. *It's over! My God, it's over!*

"Take those wet clothes off. Immediately!" Anna's voice resonated.

I spread my arm. "Anna, I'm glad to see you."

"And he's wounded again! Why don't you pay more attention, Erik? Show me it!"

She handed me a bottle and began to unwrap the pro-visory dressing.

"What's that?"

"Hot grog. It will warm you up."

"Don't you have whisky? That would do better for me."

"Sure. Your Highness, may I serve a steak with mushroom sauce and mashed potatoes?"

I chuckled. "Do you have some?"

She waved her hand and turned to Simon. "Why didn't you tell him to remove all his clothes?"

Simon shrugged. "He's a grown man. He knows what to do."

The grog was good. A wave of heat began to spread from my tummy. Anna opened the first aid kit she had brought and took out a bottle of hydrogen peroxide and a few pads. She washed the wound. I clenched my teeth and tilted my head down. The pain was worse than when the bullet scratched me. She wrapped a new dressing around my arm. The lock on the first aid kit clicked, and Anna handed me dry trousers and a jacket. "Come on! Take everything off. Your underwear, too!"

I grinned. "Do you always carry dry and clean clothes for me?"

"No. Be happy I brought them."

"I am happy."

"Then stop moaning and get changed!"

"All right, but turn away! All of you!" I said.

"Gosh! Like a child. A big grown-up child," she said but turned.

I changed, drying off with the blanket, and we went to the car. Sir Edmund Thorne, who sat on the rear seat, shook my hand.

"Thank you very much, young man!" he said.

"No need to thank, Sir. Where's Stefan?"

"Who's Stefan?" Simon said.

"The bloke who helped me."

Simon threw up his arms, shooting the questioning gaze at Anna.

"Erik," she said, "we found the body of a soldier in the Nazi uniform shot three times next to the rail track. Two shots were deadly. Could it be your Stefan?"

I said nothing, nodding. Poor Stefan. I gulped a lump that developed in my throat. Not the end he'd deserved. I remembered how he had been in his last hour. Full of energy and determination.

"Yes. Most likely, it was him. You didn't remember, Sir?" I turned to Sir Edmund Thorne.

He shook his head. "I'm sorry, young man, I didn't see his face properly."

"Erik, the dead man's face was scratched and bruised from the fall. No one could identify him."

Sadness seized my mind. I believed no tear should be spilled for any Nazi maniac. Stefan had been different, though. He hadn't been a maniac. His laughter and his sad eyes. That was how I would remember a brave man who had stepped out of his shell. In the end, he believed he should've fought for his freedom. A tear slid from my eye. I wiped it away. *Change the topic, Erik.*

"Does anyone know who stopped the train?" I said.

"I think I can explain this rather strange curiosity," the British politician said.

We all gazed at him.

"Yeah, that would also interest me," said Simon.

"I say, nothing particularly extraordinary happened. Upon observing the aeroplane in the sky, one of the guardians, in a moment of sheer trepidation, activated the emergency brake mechanism. If I interpreted their dis-course correctly, the poor chap was utterly overcome with panic. Subsequently, they proceeded to dismantle the lever, presumably to eradicate any trace of evidence. Quite the kerfuffle, I must say."

"What?!" Simon shook his head.

"That's ridiculous!" I said. "Adlerstein wanted to send me to the Nazi court because of that!"

"I do beg your pardon, my dear boy," Sir Edmund Thorne said. "The Nazi soldier maintained his vigil at the window for the entire duration. Then, in a most unseemly display, he quite lost his composure..."

Nothing could stop me from finishing his thought. "...and then shit his pants instead of taking responsibility."

I waved my hand and turned to Simon. "What happened to you? Why are you still alive?"

"Alive? You wished I was dead?" Simon said.

"No, of course not. I saw the truck explode. Can you explain that?"

"Oh, that one. The driver took a bullet in his arm, and the truck went off the road."

"Yeah and exploded. And you survived. How the hell was that possible?"

"No, the truck didn't explode. It hit a tree. Anna was following us in this automobile. We decided to put on a show for the Nazis and put a bunch of grenades into the truck tank."

"Why?"

"To fake that we died in the explosion. Is it so hard to understand?"

"Yes, it is. I don't think it was necessary. I almost died of grief." I needed to take a breath. "However, you're alive, that's what matters. What now?"

We sat in the car, I and Sir Edmund Thorne in the back. Anna started the engine.

"Now, we return to the Netherlands," Anna said.

"Nobody wants to hear what happened to me?" I said, grinning.

"You have all the time we spend on our way to Amsterdam. A train and fake documents will be waiting for John Smith. He will return to England."

I laughed. "John Smith? Come on! You must know that this man is Sir Edmund Thorne."

She turned at us, her jaw dropped. Simon looked surprised as well. The British politician's cheeks reddened.

"My sincere apologies, Miss Bakker, for my rather grievous oversight in neglecting to introduce myself properly. I trust you can appreciate the... shall we say, delicate nature of my circumstances."

She said nothing, but I knew her. She'd always hated not having all the information. Hiding something before her very eyes was the worst sin ever. Bad times for the British politician. Perhaps he would regret not finishing his journey to Berlin.

"I guess you will have to explain many things, Sir Edmund Thorne. Like what a British politician responsible for military affairs was doing in the Netherlands. Without announcing his arrival in advance." Her voice was cold and threatening.

"I assure you, Miss Bakker, that I shall elucidate the entire matter in due course. You have my solemn word as a gentleman. It is my fervent hope that, notwithstanding this trifling contretemps, our arrangement remains intact."

"Excuse me?!" Zeus wouldn't be ashamed of her voice. "I always stand by my words!"

"I assure you, Miss Bakker, I haven't the slightest inclination to question your integrity in this matter."

"Although, I believe you'll miss your train, Sir. At least until you meet with some people who will have questions. Many questions, to speak frankly."

"I am entirely cognizant of your position, Miss Bakker, and I stand prepared to elucidate the matter in its fullest detail. Naturally, certain... shall we say, sensitive aspects must remain discreet. I trust that the parties concerned will appreciate the necessity for such judicious reticence," Sir Edmund Thorne said, putting his hand on his heart and bowing slightly.

She turned away and gripped the steering wheel.

"Anna!" I said.

"What?"

"I have a wish."

"I don't have whiskey, Erik!"

"No. I want you to help me to bury Stefan."

They all kept silent for a while.

I continued. "Yes, he was in the SS, but I believe he was different. He saved my life on the train's roof and changed his..." I sighed. "Look, he deserves to be buried. I can't explain it. It's how I feel about him."

"If I may be so bold, Miss Bakker," Sir Edmund Thorne said in a low voice. "I find myself compelled to lend my modest endorsement to this young gentleman's entreaty. While I confess that the visage of his friend eludes my recollection, I am, nevertheless, indebted to them for my liberation."

Simon joined. "I think we can afford a small detour."

Anna looked at me and nodded.

Dear reader,

Thank you for buying my book. I hope you enjoyed it. I'd love it if you could post an honest review on Amazon or another book website. Getting reviews of my books gives me a big thrill, and I look forward to reading what you think. Perhaps you can mention which parts you like best or which you found terrible.

I look forward to hearing from you!
Jack Tenor

Join my mailing list for exclusive content and special offers at https://www.jacktenor.art or follow me on Facebook https://www.facebook.com/jacktenorauthor.

ABOUT THE AUTHOR

After working for decades as a software developer, Jack Tenor finally retired. The power of storytelling had always captivated him, and now that he had more free time, he felt compelled to try his hand at writing his own stories. The click-clack of the keyboard is reminiscent of his days of coding complex algorithms. But this time, instead of lines of code, he was weaving together sentences and paragraphs to create vivid narratives. He currently lives in Dublin.

Printed in Great Britain
by Amazon

57579318R00162